# NEXUS OF TIME

## A STORY OF UNSEEN STARS-2

P.CIBI SARAVANA

Made with ♥ on the Notion Press Platform
www.notionpress.com

# Contents

# Contents

# CHAPTER ONE

# THE PRICE OF SHADOWS

*In the intricately woven fabric of our contemporary global landscape, Hanjojio emerges as a singular urban tapestry, meticulously crafted to reflect the multifaceted cultural currents of our time. This metropolis, a synthesis of South Korean tenacity, Japanese elegance, Chinese tradition, and Indian vibrancy, bears a name chosen with deliberate intent. 'Han' symbolizes the indomitable spirit of South Korea, 'Jo' evokes the refined grace of Japan, 'Ji' embodies the enduring heritage of China, and 'O' resonates with the kaleidoscopic hues of India. Though an invention of fiction, Hanjojio serves as a mirror to the bustling reality of our interconnected world. Its streets teem with the vitality of diverse cultures converging and thriving, offering a vivid portrayal of unity amid diversity. Join me on a journey through the labyrinthine alleyways of Hanjojio, where the delineations between imagination and reality dissolve into an enchanting mosaic of human experience.*

## In 21$^{st}$ Century,

The city was a symphony of darkness and fury. Rain hammered against the windows, each drop a tiny fist against the glass. Lightning ripped through the sky, its jagged fingers briefly illuminating the cityscape in an eerie, ephemeral glow. Thunder roared, a primal growl that resonated through the very bones of the buildings.

Inside apartment number 111, the darkness was thick, almost palpable. The only light came from the intermittent flashes of lightning, casting fleeting shadows that danced across the walls, twisting and turning like phantoms in the gloom. The air was heavy, thick with the scent of rain and a metallic tang that seemed to cling to everything, a faint metallic whisper in the air.

Sasi Rehka, her name a whisper against the backdrop of the storm, moved with a measured, agonizing slowness. Each step was a struggle, her legs, marred with fresh wounds, buckling with a dull ache that echoed through her body. Her right hand, clutched tightly around a knife, dripped crimson onto the floor, leaving a stark, crimson trail that marked her path. She gasped, her breath catching in her throat, a ragged, painful sound swallowed by the storm outside. Her fingers, tightly clutching the knife, were slick with blood.

Tears streamed down her face, leaving glistening trails in the darkness. Her reflection in the full-length mirror, a ghostly silhouette against the flickering light, showed a woman broken. Her eyes, wide and haunted, mirrored the storm raging outside.

She reached the mirror, her hand trembling, her fingers tightening around the knife. The cold metal pressed against her skin, sending a shiver down her spine. She closed her eyes, her face a mask of despair. Her lips, tightly pressed together, were trembling. Her brow was furrowed, the lines etched deep with pain. Her face was a portrait of anguish and resignation, a silent plea for the storm to end.

Outside the door, a group of figures stood silhouetted against the lightning flashes. They were cloaked in darkness, their faces obscured by shadows, but their forms were unmistakable. The gleam of weapons, a glint of steel in the dim light, revealed their menacing intent. They waited, their silence as palpable as the storm itself, a chilling tableau of shadows and steel.

Sasi's breath hitched, her body convulsing with a shuddering sob. Her throat tightened, the words caught in her throat, a choked lament for a life shattered.

"Why... Why did it all come to this?" The words were barely audible, choked by the sobs that racked her body. "It's all my fault. I'm responsible... I had no choice. I lost everything. There's nothing left..."

The camera panned to the storm-tossed sky. The wind, a living entity, tore at the clouds, creating a swirling vortex of darkness and fury. A voice, calm and measured, cut through the roar of the storm.

"Every choice has a consequence. Every word, every action, weaves a tapestry of fate. We must face the consequences, no matter how daunting they may seem." The voice paused, allowing the silence to amplify the weight of its words. "Now, let us rewind the clock. Let us delve into the past, to unravel the story of how this night was born."

The scene dissolved, leaving the storm raging on, the echoes of Sasi's despair fading with the wind. But the question lingered, a dark whisper in the storm's roar: what events led to this moment of despair? What choices, what actions, had woven this tapestry of tragedy?

# CHAPTER TWO

# A New Game Begins

*In cosmic relam,*

The assistant, a young man with a mischievous glint in his eye, sprawled across a cloud, its surface soft as down. He idly plucked a plump grape from a cluster beside him, the scent of ripe fruit filling the air, and popped it into his mouth. He savored the sweet burst of juice, a contented smile playing on his lips. He was lost in his reverie, completely absorbed in the moment.

But his tranquil state was shattered. The cloud beneath him shuddered, a subtle tremor that sent a shiver through his body. He sat up, his dreamy expression replaced by a flicker of anxiety. He knew that feeling. The unmistakable tremor that accompanied the Elder God's arrival.

He tossed the half-eaten apple aside, its trajectory a perfect arc towards the ground. He scrambled to his feet, his fingers fumbling as he reached for the Book of Fate. His eyes darted frantically around the cloud, his movements a flurry of nervous energy. With a frantic rustle of pages, he flipped through the ancient tome, desperately trying to appear busy.

The Elder God materialized before him, a majestic figure cloaked in shimmering robes. The air shimmered with his arrival, a palpable shift in the fabric of the cosmos. His robes, woven from starlight, pulsed with an otherworldly luminescence. He surveyed the scene with a knowing gaze, his eyes lingering on the discarded apple.

He picked it up, a wry smile playing on his lips. "Hmmm, child," he said, his voice a low rumble that resonated with ancient wisdom. "What are you doing? Eating and resting? Avoiding your work, are we? I see you like this apple."

The assistant, caught red-handed, froze. His usually confident voice faltered, becoming a mere whisper. "Oh, Great One, greetings... I... I was lost in thought... I forgot my work... Forgive me, Great One." He bowed his head, his cheeks flushing crimson.

The Elder God's smile remained unchanged, his gaze steady and unwavering. "Let's not repeat this," he said, the playful reprimand laced with a hint of warning.

Relieved by the lack of harshness, the assistant straightened his posture, a desperate attempt to regain his composure. "Great One," he asked, trying to sound nonchalant, "what brings you here?"

The Elder God's smile deepened, his eyes twinkling with amusement. "Child, have you forgotten what I said before?"

The assistant's face contorted with the effort of recollection. A flicker of understanding dawning on him. "Great One," he said, a sense of realization in his voice, "I remember now. You said there are others who need our help, is that correct?"

"Correct, child," the Elder God confirmed, his voice a low hum that echoed across the cosmos.

"Great One," the assistant said, his voice tinged with anxiety, "the last time we explored a world, it was fantasy, right? This time, it's another fantasy-based story, but even more complicated, a long journey..."

The Elder God chuckled softly, his laughter echoing through the cosmos. "Child, child, I know what happened last time. A bit too much fantasy, wasn't it? How about a sci-fi adventure this time? Shall we explore that?"

The assistant's eyes widened, his shock palpable. "Sci-fi? Are you serious, Great One? But... okay, Great One. Who is this person, and what is their story?"

The Elder God raised his hand, a surge of power emanating from him. With a flick of his wrist, he transported the Book of Fate into the assistant's hands. The pages of the book shimmered, then began to grow, expanding with an ethereal glow. The assistant, wide-eyed, stared at the unfolding pages.

"We will explore the story of a girl named Sasi," the Elder God said, his voice resonating with anticipation. "She is trapped, playing with time, facing the consequences of her actions. In the realm of sci-fi, we shall play this game once again."

"Okay, let's begin this game," the assistant said, a flicker of excitement replacing his nervousness. "I hope this journey will be interesting."

The Book of Fate pulsed with light, the pages continuing to grow, a portal to a new adventure unfolding. The scene faded, leaving the Elder God and the assistant standing in the cosmic realm, ready to embark on another tale of fate, this time within the framework of science fiction.

# CHAPTER THREE

# The Weight of Expectations

*In 2050,*

The city was a tapestry of motion, a vibrant symphony of steel and glass. The morning sun, a pale disc struggling through the smog, cast a hazy glow over the bustling streets. People swarmed the sidewalks, their faces etched with a mixture of determination and exhaustion, their footsteps a rhythmic beat against the concrete. Towering skyscrapers, their surfaces shimmering with a thousand reflections, reached for the sky, symbols of ambition and progress.

In the heart of this urban jungle, nestled amongst the towering structures, stood a haven of peace. A sprawling mansion, its facade a blend of traditional elegance and modern futurism, exuded an air of quiet luxury. A meticulously manicured garden, a vibrant explosion of color against the gray concrete of the city, surrounded the house. Here, amidst the fragrant roses and the delicate petals of orchids, a team of robotic gardeners, their movements precise and efficient, tended to the flora with meticulous care.

Inside, the house was a testament to both technology and tradition. The interior, a seamless blend of sleek lines and timeless elegance, showcased the latest advancements in home automation. Walls shimmered with holographic displays, showcasing stunning works of art that seemed to pulse with life. Sunlight streamed through vast windows, illuminating gleaming surfaces and throwing playful shadows on the polished floors.

In the kitchen, Kira(50), a woman whose face bore the marks of time with a quiet grace, moved with a practiced ease. Her movements were fluid, her hands a blur of motion as she prepared a cup of coffee. Beside her, Rox, a sleek, silver robotic assistant with eyes that glowed with an ethereal blue light, moved with a silent efficiency, its metallic arm extending to adjust the temperature of the coffee machine.

"Thank you, Rox," Kira said, her voice a gentle melody.

"You're welcome, Mrs. Kira," Rox responded, its voice a soothing synthesized tone.

Kira left the kitchen, her steps carrying her up the grand staircase. She paused outside a door, the handle gleaming with a cool, metallic sheen. Within the room, her son, Yash(25), a young man of twenty-five, lay sprawled on a plush bed, his face relaxed in slumber.

Kira approached the bed, her footsteps silent on the plush carpet. She placed the steaming cup of coffee on the bedside table, the aroma of freshly brewed coffee filling the air.

"Wake up, sweetheart," she said softly, her voice laced with a mother's love. "It's morning."

Yash stirred, a groan escaping his lips. "Please, Mom, let me sleep five more minutes."

"Wake up, Yash. Have your coffee," Kira urged, her tone a little firmer.

Yash remained unresponsive, his breathing shallow and even. Kira stood there, her gaze lingering on her son's face. A mixture of concern and a quiet sense of worry lingered in her eyes.

Then, Rox's synthesized voice cut through the silence. "Mr. Yash, wake up. Mr. Dev is coming to your room."

Yash's eyes snapped open, his sleepiness melting away in an instant. He sat up, his movements jerky as he rubbed the sleep from his eyes. Rox, ever efficient, extended its arm, its metallic fingers deftly manipulating Yash's clothes, helping him to change and freshen up. Kira watched with a soft smile, a mother's pride filling her heart.

The door opened, and Yash's father, Dev(50), a man who exuded a quiet strength, entered the room.

"Hey, Yash, wake up," Dev said, his voice filled with warmth. "Come, let's have breakfast."

"Yes, Dad," Yash responded, his voice still thick with sleep.

"You too, dear," Dev said, turning to Kira. "Come with Yash to the dining table."

Yash took a sip of the coffee, the bitter taste instantly rousing him from his slumber. He joined his parents at the dining table, where a lavish breakfast had been prepared. Kira busied herself, serving Dev and watching with a quiet satisfaction as they ate.

Dev, ever attentive, noticed Kira's silent efforts. "Sit, dear. Why are you always putting all the work on your head? You need to rest well, eat healthily, and take care of yourself." He paused, his gaze meeting hers. "After all, you are my wife."

Yash, seated opposite his parents, watched the exchange with a mixture of affection and a touch of annoyance.

"Come on, Dad, Mom," he said, trying to lighten the mood. "Not at the breakfast table."

Dev chuckled, a soft sound that belied a hint of concern. "Sorry, son," he said, his gaze turning to Yash. "I need to ask you something."

Yash stopped eating, his gaze meeting his father's. "What's the matter, Dad?"

"Nothing," Dev said, a flicker of worry crossing his face. "I know you've been working hard to get the green signal for your project."

Yash's face fell. "Yes, Dad," he said, his voice a low murmur.

"And you have your project presentation today, right?" Dev asked.

Yash's eyes widened. "Oh, yes, Dad, I forgot," he said, his voice laced with panic. He abruptly stood up, pushing his chair back with a clatter.

"See you, Dad, Mom," he said, rushing toward the door.

"But Yash, wait," Kira called out, her voice laced with concern. "We have something else to talk to you about."

But Yash was gone, his footsteps echoing through the house as he raced out the door.

"Rox," he called, his voice tinged with desperation, "How much time is left? Tell me the fastest route."

Rox, the robotic assistant, projected a holographic image of the fastest route, the time remaining flashing in bold red letters.

Yash wasted no time. He mounted his sleek, futuristic motorcycle and roared out of the garage, his engine a powerful growl that echoed through the quiet streets.

Dev, his gaze following Yash's departure, turned to Kira, a worried frown etched on his face.

"Dear, I'm starting to worry about his future," he said, his voice laced with a father's concern.

"Why, dear?" Kira asked, her hand reaching out to take his.

"He's worked so hard for this day," Dev said. "He's been passionate about this project since he was a boy. He's been rejected by so many government officials. I hope this time, he succeeds."

Kira squeezed his hand, her gaze filled with a quiet strength. "Dear, I have something else to say," she said, her voice soft but firm.

Dev turned to her, his eyes filled with a mixture of curiosity and apprehension.

"He's getting older," Kira said, her voice barely a whisper. "Perhaps we should start arranging a marriage for him. If he had a woman by his side, his life would be luckier."

Dev's expression shifted, a mixture of worry and doubt clouding his features. "What if that girl turns out to be his unlucky charm?" he asked, his voice tinged with a hint of skepticism.

Kira hesitated, her gaze searching his. "Perhaps it's time we let fate take its course," she said, a gentle smile gracing her lips. "Let him come home after his project presentation. Then we can talk about it."

Dev nodded, a quiet sigh escaping his lips. He turned and walked towards his study, leaving Kira to stand there, her gaze lingering on a photograph of Yash that hung on the wall. The smile on his face, captured in the photograph, was a stark contrast to the worry that shadowed his mother's eyes.

This was the beginning of a new chapter in their lives, a chapter filled with uncertainty and the weight of expectations. As Yash raced towards his project presentation, his parents were left to grapple with the complexities of love, ambition, and the delicate dance of fate.

# CHAPTER FOUR

# THE NEXUS OF DREAMS

The presentation hall buzzed with anticipation. Rows of investors, scientists, and high-ranking officials sat around sleek, circular tables, their faces a mixture of curiosity and skepticism. The air hummed with a low, electric tension. A sense of excitement hung in the air, tinged with a cautious undercurrent of doubt.

Yash stood at the head of the room, his shoulders slumped slightly beneath the weight of expectation. His eyes, usually bright with passion, held a flicker of uncertainty.

"Sorry, sir," he said, his voice a little shaky, "I'm late."

The investor, a man with a sharp, calculating gaze, waved dismissively. "It's okay, Mr. Yash," he said, his tone clipped. "Now explain your project."

Yash took a deep breath, his fingers tracing the sleek lines of a small, silver device that lay on the table before him. He activated his AI assistant, Rox, a sleek, silver orb that hovered above his palm.

"Rox, activate the projection," Yash commanded.

The orb hummed, and a holographic projection unfolded in the center of the room. A three-dimensional image of a sleek, futuristic wristwatch shimmered into existence, its intricate design captivating the attention of everyone in the room. Heads tilted, eyes narrowed as they examined the image, a mixture of awe and skepticism playing across their faces.

"Ladies and gentlemen," Yash began, his voice gaining confidence as he spoke, "I present to you my dream project – Nexus, a time travel watch."

A collective gasp rippled through the room. A scientist, his brow furrowed, leaned forward. "A time travel watch, Mr. Yash? How is that possible? Even in this day and age, scientists across the globe are struggling to invent a time machine. You claim to have a blueprint?"

Yash's gaze met the scientist's, his eyes burning with a fierce determination. "Yes, sir," he said, his voice unwavering. "This is my lifelong dream project. I've been working on this since I was a child. All I need is your permission to execute it, sir."

The investor, his gaze fixed on the holographic projection, tapped his fingers thoughtfully against the table. "This project looks good," he said, his voice measured, "but what if it causes problems? We can't play with time. And why did you name it Nexus?"

Yash's smile held a glimmer of hope. "Sir, I chose the name Nexus because it means joining. This device will join time and humanity, allowing people to use it safely. It will create a balance between time and the user, the wearer becoming a nexus being between the two."

The room erupted in a low hum of discussion. The scientists argued amongst themselves, their voices a symphony of skepticism and intrigue. The investors, their eyes narrowed, weighed the potential risks and rewards. Yash watched them, his nervousness growing with each passing second. He was a young man on the precipice of fulfilling his dream, yet his heart sank with every passing moment.

Finally, the investor, his expression grim, stood up, followed by the other members of the panel.

"Sorry, Mr. Yash," the investor said, his voice devoid of emotion. "I understand you have an innovative project, but we cannot sponsor it or give permission for its execution."

His words were like a punch to the gut. The room emptied as the investors and officials filed out, leaving Yash alone, his dreams shattered. He sank into the chair, his shoulders slumping with defeat. His fingers clenched into fists, his face contorted with a mixture of anger and despair. He reached for a stack of papers on the table and flung them across the room, the sound of their impact echoing in the silence.

"Calm down, Mr. Yash," Rox said, its synthesized voice a calming presence in the room. "Please."

"What am I going to do?" Yash cried out, his voice thick with frustration. "This is my life's work! All of this, wasted in one day! Am I really an unlucky person? I just need a chance to prove myself."

He started to sob, the pent-up emotions finally breaking through.

"Mr. Yash, Mr. Yash, you have a call from your mother, Mrs. Kira," Rox announced, its voice devoid of emotion, yet a beacon of comfort in the storm of Yash's despair.

Yash wiped his tears, his head bowed. He stood up, his legs wobbly, and walked out of the hall, his shoulders slumped, his heart heavy with disappointment. The hallways of the building seemed to stretch endlessly before him, a reflection of the vast chasm of despair that had opened up within him.

He walked down the street, his eyes fixed on the pavement, his thoughts consumed by the crushing weight of his failure. The city, once a source of hope and ambition, now felt like a cold, indifferent observer. He had come so close to fulfilling his dreams, yet he was now further away than ever before.

He had to get home, to his parents, to seek solace in their love and support. He just hoped that they could offer him the strength he needed to pick himself up, to find the courage to keep dreaming.

# CHAPTER FIVE

# A Calculated Chance

The grand hall of Yash's home felt strangely suffocating. Yash slumped onto the plush sofa, his head bowed, his shoulders slumped with defeat. The air hung heavy, thick with the silence of a dream deferred. He reached out, his fingers tracing the worn leather of the sofa, a futile attempt to ground himself, to find solace in the familiar.

Kira entered the room, a vision of quiet strength, her face etched with worry. In her hand, she held a glass of chilled juice, its condensation a fleeting reminder of the warmth she longed to instill in her son.

"Don't worry, my sweetheart," Kira said, her voice laced with a gentle reassurance, her gaze lingering on Yash's slumped form.

Yash's head snapped up, his eyes filled with a desperate plea. "Why, Mom? Why is this happening to me? Am I that unlucky?" His voice, usually filled with a youthful optimism, crackled with frustration.

Kira, her heart aching for her son, moved towards him, her steps slow and measured. She placed the glass of juice on the coffee table, the clink of glass against wood a sharp contrast to the silence that enveloped the room.

She then gently enveloped him in a warm embrace, her arms a comforting haven against the storm raging within him. Yash leaned into her, his body seeking solace in her presence.

"Yash, listen," Kira said, her voice a soothing balm. "If our plans don't work out today, it doesn't mean the plan is bad. It just means our time isn't right now. Wait, and time will make everything alright. Remember, everything has its own time, and great things take time."

Kira's words, laced with wisdom and love, began to seep into Yash's troubled mind. He slowly pulled away from his mother's embrace, his face still etched with sadness, but the despair seemed to have lifted slightly. He stood up, his movements sluggish, and turned to head towards his room.

"Yash, wait a moment," Kira said, her voice a quiet, but firm command.

Yash paused, turning back to face his mother. His eyes, still filled with uncertainty, met hers.

Kira, a knowing smile on her lips, reached into her purse and pulled out a white envelope, its edges slightly curled. She handed it to Yash.

"Yash, I want you to look at this."

Yash took the envelope, his fingers fumbling as he opened it. The paper rustled, the sound a stark contrast to the silence of the room. Inside, he found a wedding invitation, its surface adorned with delicate floral patterns. His eyes scanned the printed text, his heart skipping a beat as he recognized his own name, printed alongside another: "Yash and Sasi Rekha weds."

He stared at the invitation, his mind reeling. His breath caught in his throat, and a silent gasp escaped his lips. This was a surprise, a complete shock, and one he was ill-prepared to receive.

"Mom...," Yash started, his voice trembling.

"Please, my sweetheart," Kira interrupted, her voice laced with a mixture of desperation and hope. "Just do this for me. This girl, Sasi, is a wonderful person. She's brilliant, kind, and energetic. She has a single mother, her father passed away before she was even born. Please, Yash, accept this offer. Maybe, just maybe, your life will be better after this marriage."

Yash remained silent, his mind racing, torn between his own desires and his mother's heartfelt plea.

"Mom, I don't want to get married now," he said, his voice a low murmur. "Please understand."

He started to argue, to plead with his mother, but his words were swallowed by the sudden entrance of Dev, his father.

"Yash," Dev said, his voice firm but laced with concern, "lower your voice. It's not right to yell at your mother. She's only doing this for you."

"But Dad..." Yash began, his voice filled with frustration.

"Listen, Yash," Dev said, placing a comforting hand on his shoulder. "Just accept it. Take this."

Dev reached into his pocket and pulled out a photograph, its edges slightly worn. He handed it to Yash.

Yash hesitantly took the photo and unfolded it. He stared at the image, his gaze fixed on the woman in the picture. Sasi Rekha was beautiful, her features delicate yet strong, her eyes radiating a quiet confidence. The photograph, a simple yet captivating image, seemed to hold a powerful energy.

Dev and Kira watched him, their faces filled with anticipation, their hope tinged with a sense of desperation.

"Yash, what do you think?" Kira asked, her voice barely a whisper. "Do you like her? Are you ready?"

Yash stared at the photograph, his heart racing, his mind racing through a whirlwind of emotions. He met his parents' gaze, his eyes filled with a mixture of reluctance and a faint glimmer of curiosity.

"Ok, Mom, Dad," he said, his voice a low murmur. "I'll accept this marriage for you both."

Kira and Dev erupted in a wave of joy. Kira enveloped Yash in a warm hug, her tears a mixture of relief and happiness. Yash, his initial resistance melting away, returned her hug, his own heart softened by his mother's affection.

Dev, a smile beaming across his face, watched them with a father's pride.

"Ok, everything is alright now," Dev declared, his voice booming with enthusiasm. "Let's start the marriage celebrations!"

Rox, ever observant, watched the exchange unfold, its blue eyes fixated on the photograph of Sasi.

"Mr. Yash, you are so lucky," Rox said, its synthesized voice laced with a hint of amusement. "I have a feeling that she will bring many good things to your life after your marriage. She's like a lucky star."

Yash, his face a mixture of nervousness and a forced smile, shot Rox a look of annoyance.

"Oh, good, never mind, Mr. Yash," Rox quickly added, its tone shifting from amusement to a more cautious neutrality.

Yash, his mind a jumble of conflicting emotions, stood there, caught between a wave of anxiety and a flicker of cautious hope. He was about to embark on a new chapter in his life, a chapter that was not of his own choosing, a chapter that was driven by the hopes and desires of his parents, and a chapter that promised a life shared with a woman he barely knew. But he couldn't deny the slight glimmer of anticipation that flickered within him, a whisper of possibility, of a chance at a new beginning. He was about to marry Sasi Rekha, and his future, like the swirling storm outside, was uncertain, unpredictable, and full of potential.

# CHAPTER SIX

# A New Dawn, A Distant Heart

The marriage preparations commenced with grandeur. Yash, clad in a resplendent groom's attire, walked to the stage accompanied by his parents, Kira and Dev. On the opposite side, Sasi, radiant in her elegant bridal dress, ascended the stage with a serene smile that illuminated her face accompanied by her mother Zara. Yash's expression was a mixture of reluctance and resignation, but Sasi's calmness and happiness shone through. As they stood together, exchanging vows, Yash remained distant, while Sasi's joy remained undimmed.

The next morning, Kira headed to the kitchen to prepare coffee for her son and herself. To her surprise, she found the coffee already made. Sasi stood there, a gentle smile on her face, holding a cup of coffee for her mother-in-law. Kira's heart warmed as she took the coffee, savoring both the drink and the thoughtfulness behind it.

Sasi, carrying another cup, walked gracefully to Yash's room, where he was still asleep. She placed the coffee on the table and stood silently, her expression gentle and hopeful. From outside the room, through the window, Kira and Dev watched the scene unfold.

"Mr. Yash, wake up," Rox's AI voice chimed, followed by the sound of the alarm.

Yash stirred, his eyes opening to see Sasi standing by his side, a smile playing on her lips.

"Good morning, dear," Sasi said softly, extending the coffee towards him. "Have a coffee."

Yash glanced at her and then at the coffee before taking it. He sipped it silently, his face devoid of any warmth.

"How is the coffee?" Sasi asked, her voice tinged with a hint of hope.

Yash continued drinking, showing no sign of appreciation. "The coffee is okay, but I thought Mom would give me this."

Sasi's heart sank at his words, and she watched as Yash got up and went to the washroom. Outside, Kira and Dev shared a look of concern, feeling Sasi's pain.

Kira met Sasi in the hallway. "Don't feel disheartened, dear. Yash will understand you soon. Just give him time."

Sasi nodded, holding back her tears. "I understand. Thank you, Mother."

Dev sighed, watching Sasi walk away. "I'm worried about her," he said softly.

A few minutes later, at the dining table, Yash sat down for breakfast. Sasi approached him with a dish she had prepared, hoping to please him. Yash, however, ignored her efforts and chose another dish. Sasi's heart ached, but she remained silent.

Before leaving the house, Yash asked for his overcoat. Sasi quickly went upstairs to fetch it, but by the time she returned, a robot maid had already assisted him with the help of Rox's AI. Yash left without acknowledging her, and Sasi stood there, feeling a deep sense of worry.

Kira and Dev, who had been observing the entire situation, approached Sasi.

"I'm sorry, dear, for his behavior," Kira said gently.

"It's okay," Sasi replied, forcing a smile. "It's not his fault. Like you said, he needs time to understand me."

Dev placed a reassuring hand on Sasi's shoulder. "Yes, but he won't be himself until his dream succeeds."

Sasi looked at him, curiosity piqued. "His dream? What is it, Father-in-law?"

Dev and Kira explained Yash's lifelong aspiration and the recent disappointment he faced.

"Oh, I see. So, this is the reason he's upset," Sasi said, her understanding deepening. "Thank you both for telling me."

Kira smiled warmly. "Don't worry, dear. We both know how to handle him. When he returns, spend time together. It will help him understand you."

"Thank you, Mother. Thank you, Father," Sasi said, bowing respectfully. She looked at the front door where Yash had left, her heart filled with determination and a gentle smile on her face as she watched the sun rise over the beautiful garden.

# CHAPTER SEVEN

# A FORCED OUTING

The evening air was thick with the scent of honeysuckle and the faint hum of the city, a stark contrast to the peaceful serenity of the mansion. Kira, her gaze fixed on the front door, watched as her son, Yash, returned home.

"Yash, you're back," she said, her voice laced with relief.

"Yeah, Mom," Yash responded, his voice a little strained. He sank onto the plush sofa, his shoulders slumping with a weariness that went beyond the day's events.

"Yash, you have another job to do," Dev said, his voice firm, his gaze unwavering.

Yash looked at his father, his brow furrowed with confusion.

"Take your wife out," Dev continued. "Spend some time together outside, relax. You'll find the relaxation you're looking for."

Yash's expression shifted, a mixture of annoyance and reluctance replacing the initial confusion. "But Dad..." he began.

"Please, Yash," Kira interjected, her voice gentle but insistent. "Spend time with your wife. She's waiting for you upstairs."

Yash sighed, his shoulders slumping further. "Alright, Mom, Dad. I'll take her out."

He headed towards the grand staircase, his footsteps echoing through the hall, his movements heavy with a sense of resignation.

Upstairs, Sasi, her face radiating a warmth that was at odds with Yash's dejected mood, waited for him. She had dressed for an evening out, a simple yet elegant ensemble that highlighted her natural beauty.

"Dear, shall we go?" Sasi asked, her voice laced with a gentle hope that was almost palpable.

"Yes, come," Yash responded, his tone curt, his movements stiff. He gesture toward the door, his expression as cold as the evening air.

Sasi, undeterred by his demeanor, reached for a black and violet overcoat, its fabric soft and luxurious. She held it out to Yash.

"Here, wear this," she said. "It's beautiful and perfect for you."

Yash glanced at the coat, his eyes momentarily caught by the intricate design, but he quickly shook his head. "It's nice, but I think the dress I'm wearing is fine for going out. Let's go," he said, his tone clipped, his eyes avoiding hers.

Sasi, her heart sinking with each rejection, managed a smile. She was glad that he was taking her out, even if it felt forced.

Before they left, Yash turned to Sasi. "Here, take this," he said, his voice almost apologetic. He handed her a delicate silver bracelet, its surface gleaming with a soft, blue light.

Sasi took the bracelet, her fingers tracing the smooth lines. Her eyes widened as she noticed the small, silver orb that sat nestled within the bracelet.

"Rox," a synthesized voice echoed, its tones smooth and comforting. "Hello, Mrs. Sasi. Greetings. I am Rox, the AI. I am your AI companion."

Sasi, taken aback by the sudden introduction, looked at the bracelet, her eyes wide with surprise and a hint of wonder.

"Thank you," she managed, a gentle smile gracing her lips. She tried to speak, to ask about the AI, but Yash interrupted.

"It's getting late, let's go," he said, his tone curt, and without waiting for a response, he turned and headed downstairs.

Sasi, her heart a mixture of anticipation and uncertainty, followed him, her gaze lingering on the bracelet, the small blue orb pulsating with a faint light.

Downstairs, Yash stood by the front door, his back to her, his posture rigid. Sasi, walking behind him, heard Rox's voice again.

"Don't worry, Mrs. Sasi," Rox said, its voice a soothing balm. "Mr. Yash will understand you soon."

"Yeah," Sasi whispered, her voice barely audible. "Hey, Rox, don't call me too formal. Just call me Sasi, alright."

"Okay, Sasi," Rox responded, displaying a holographic emoji of a smiling face.

Sasi, touched by the AI's gesture, couldn't help but smile.

She hurried down the stairs, her heart pounding with a mixture of hope and trepidation. She reached the landing just as Yash was opening the front door, his back turned towards her. She paused, her eyes searching his.

She felt a pang of apprehension as she remembered the coldness in his gaze.

She had to convince him that this outing was a step towards a new beginning.

"Yash, wait," she said, her voice laced with a quiet determination.

She quickly turned back towards the staircase, a sudden feeling of urgency propelling her forward. She knew she had to talk to Kira and Dev, to gain their support, to reassure herself that her journey with Yash was not over.

# A New Beginning, A Distant Echo

"Sasi, my dear," Kira said, her voice warm and welcoming. "You're like our daughter now. Think of us as your mother and father."

Sasi, her eyes glistening with tears, embraced Kira and Dev. She felt a sense of comfort and acceptance in their presence, a sense of belonging that had been missing in her life.

Yash, his face still expressionless, stood waiting by the front door.

"Come, let's go," he said, his tone curt, his gaze unwavering. "We'll take the car."

Sasi, her heart heavy with a mixture of hope and apprehension, followed him.

"But I thought we were going on your bike," she said, her voice a soft murmur. Her expression shifted, a flicker of disappointment passing across her face.

Kira and Dev, watching from inside the house, exchanged a worried glance.

The car, a sleek, futuristic model, hummed to life. Yash, seated behind the wheel, looked straight ahead, his jaw clenched, his expression cold and distant. Sasi, sitting beside him, felt a chill pass through her.

The drive was silent, the only sounds the hum of the engine and the rhythmic thrumming of the tires on the road. Yash, his focus entirely on the road, ignored her completely. Sasi, unable to bear the silence and the tension, turned her gaze to the window, watching the cityscape blur past.

They spent the evening at a luxurious restaurant, a bustling theme park, and a quiet, deserted beach. Throughout it all, Yash remained distant, his responses curt, his eyes avoiding hers. Sasi felt a deep sense of loneliness, a growing sense of despair, her initial hope fading with every passing moment.

As the sun dipped below the horizon, painting the sky in hues of orange and purple, Yash turned the car towards home.

Sasi, her heart heavy with disappointment, silently followed him.

She had hoped for a chance to connect with her husband, to build a foundation for their future, but the evening had only confirmed her fears.

They reached the mansion, and as Sasi stepped out of the car, Kira met her.

"Sasi, my dear," Kira said, her voice filled with concern, "how did you enjoy your evening? Did you spend time together?"

Sasi's face, a reflection of her internal turmoil, was dull, a stark contrast to the vibrant glow of the sunset.

Kira, sensing the truth behind Sasi's quiet demeanor, simply offered a comforting smile.

"It's alright, my dear," she said, her voice laced with reassurance. "It takes time."

As Yash entered the house, his phone rang. He answered, his face instantly transforming as he listened.

"Hello?" he said, his voice a mixture of disbelief and elation. "Yes, sir... We're sorry to disturb you... Yes, sir, what is it?"

Sasi, her heart pounding with a mixture of hope and trepidation, turned towards her room. She couldn't bear to hear the conversation.

Yash's voice, a mix of awe and excitement, echoed through the hall.

"Yes, sir... I understand... We've received an order to approve the project from the higher officer's recommendation. His name is V."

Yash's parents, their faces alight with joy, exchanged a knowing glance.

"Yes sir... I don't know what to say..."

Sasi, her curiosity piqued, paused just outside her door, her hand hovering over the handle.

"Mr. Yash, we've thought about your project Nexus again," the voice on the other side of the phone said. "The higher officer, Mr. V, has taken the responsibility for the project. He has confidence in you. And yes, Mr. V has approved the project."

Yash, his eyes wide with disbelief, his hands trembling with a mixture of shock and excitement, let out a gasp.

"Thank you, sir, thank you so much," Yash said, his voice laced with gratitude. "I don't know what to say."

"It's alright, Mr. Yash," the investor's voice said. "Mr. V is on vacation with his family. He'll contact you soon. He wants to say good luck on the project."

Yash, his emotions bubbling over, dropped to his knees, his face awash with joy and tears. He stood up, his eyes bright, his smile wide, and ran towards his parents, his heart overflowing with a sense of triumph.

"Mom, Dad, I got the approval," Yash exclaimed, his voice filled with excitement. "The project Nexus, it's approved!"

Kira and Dev, their faces beaming with pride, embraced their son.

"Yash, you should tell Sasi," Dev said, his voice filled with warmth.

Yash's smile faltered, his eyes momentarily glancing towards the closed door of Sasi's room.

"Why, Dad?" he asked, a mischievous glint in his eyes.

"Yash, what are you saying?" Kira said, her tone laced with a mixture of amusement and exasperation. "We told you she was lucky for you. See, after you married her, your dream came true."

Yash laughed, a light, playful sound that was music to his parents' ears.

"Mom," he said, a teasing smirk on his lips. "Nice joke. She didn't do anything. And I was lucky to marry her? This success was all because of my hard work and Mr. V."

Sasi, standing just outside her room, heard his words. A flicker of hurt crossed her face, but she quickly masked it with a smile. She was happy for her husband, thrilled that his dream was finally coming true.

"Okay, Mom, Dad," Yash said, his voice filled with excitement. "My dream is coming true tomorrow. The project Nexus is finally happening."

He turned and headed towards his room, his footsteps echoing through the silent house.

"Oh, dear," Dev said, his voice laced with a mixture of confusion and admiration. "I can't understand him. He has such a different perspective, a different mindset."

Kira chuckled, her eyes twinkling with amusement. "Why are you saying that?" she asked. "He's exactly like you, dear. Like father, like son. His personality is just your younger version."

Dev, a slight smile playing on his lips, looked at Kira, his heart filled with a mixture of pride and a touch of wistfulness. He couldn't help but feel a twinge of guilt for the way he had treated his son, the way he had burdened him with his own expectations, but the joy of seeing his son's dreams come true filled him with a sense of overwhelming happiness.

Their family, united by love and a shared history, was on the cusp of a new beginning. The future, once shrouded in uncertainty, now shimmered with the promise of hope and a chance for new beginnings.

# CHAPTER NINE

# THE PRICE OF NEGLECT

Days bled into weeks, weeks into months. The walls of Yash's lab had become his world. He lived and breathed amongst the intricate mechanisms of the Nexus watch, his mind a whirlwind of calculations, schematics, and the intoxicating promise of his ambition. He traced lines of code with a laser pointer, his eyes glued to the holographic projections of swirling time currents, his fingers flying across the keyboard, driven by a feverish desire to complete his masterpiece. The hum of the lab's equipment, the rhythmic glow of the screens, the symphony of clicking keys, they were the only sounds he truly knew.

He was oblivious to the silence that had settled upon his home. His phone, once a lifeline to his family, lay forgotten on his workbench, its screen cracked from a careless toss. He hadn't noticed the unanswered calls and texts, the messages from Sasi, each one a whisper of concern and a plea for connection. He hadn't seen the worried faces of his parents, the unspoken questions in their eyes. The world outside the lab, with its mundane routines and the gentle rhythm of human lives, had faded into a distant memory.

One evening, the lab's lights reflected in his tired eyes. His fingers, stained with a mixture of grease and caffeine, gently traced the sleek lines of the Nexus watch, now complete. The watch, a testament to his dedication, rested on the workbench, a tangible manifestation of his dreams. But as he stared at the silver surface, a shadow of guilt crept across his features.

He felt a tremor in his chest, a sudden pang of awareness. He remembered the warmth of Sasi's smile, the sound of his parents' laughter, the comforting weight of their presence. He had pushed them all away, his mind consumed by the promise of the watch, the potential for power beyond his wildest imaginings.

The air in the lab seemed to grow heavy. He felt the weight of his neglect pressing upon him, a suffocating pressure. He picked up his phone, its cool metal sending a shiver down his spine. He hesitated. His fingers trembled slightly as he dialed the familiar number.

Days bled into weeks, weeks into months. Yash's world revolved around the intricate mechanisms of the Nexus watch, his mind a whirlwind of calculations, schematics, and the intoxicating promise of his ambition. His days were consumed by the lab, his nights filled with restless sleep punctuated by dreams of swirling time currents and the pulsating energy of a universe bending to his will.

He was oblivious to the void that his absence created. His phone, once a lifeline to his family, became a tool of avoidance. His mind, fixated on the grand vision of his project, ignored the quiet whispers of his heart. He hadn't visited home, hadn't spent a moment with his wife, hadn't even noticed her attempts to reach out. His focus was a laser beam, focused solely on the gleaming watch that promised to rewrite the very fabric of reality.

The air in the lab hummed with a strange energy, a palpable tension that seemed to emanate from the intricate circuits and glowing screens that surrounded Yash. He worked tirelessly, driven by a feverish desire to complete his masterpiece. The world outside the lab, with its mundane routines and the gentle rhythm of human lives, had become a distant echo, a faded memory.

"Yes," he breathed, his eyes fixed on the watch resting on the workbench. "Finally, the watch is ready." He smiled, a fleeting, triumphant expression that illuminated his face.

He picked up the watch, its silver surface gleaming under the lab's fluorescent lights. It was the culmination of his years of toil, a tangible manifestation of his dreams. But a sudden pang of guilt, a whisper of a forgotten responsibility, touched his heart. He had neglected his wife, his family, in his pursuit of this grand ambition.

He needed to share his success, to tell his investors, to announce the world-altering implications of his creation.

He hurried to a private room in the lab, the door closing behind him with a soft click. He picked up his phone, his fingers trembling slightly as he dialed the familiar number.

# CHAPTER TEN

# THE ECHO OF TIME

Meanwhile, at his home, the mansion seemed to echo with a quiet sadness. Sasi, her heart heavy with the weight of Yash's absence, busied herself in the grand hall, arranging a plate of assorted delicacies on the coffee table.

Kira, her face a reflection of her son's absence, entered the room.

"Sasi, dear," Kira said, her voice filled with concern. "Why are you doing this?"

"Nothing," Sasi responded, her voice soft, her eyes downcast. "Yash hasn't visited home in days. I'm worried about him."

Kira, her heart aching for her son and her new daughter-in-law, moved towards Sasi.

"Is that your problem?" she said, her voice laced with understanding. "Okay, if you miss him, go to his lab and see him. Take the food with you."

A sudden wave of joy washed over Sasi. She immediately began to pack the food into a stylish, futuristic lunchbox.

Sasi, her eyes filled with a newfound hope, turned to Kira and Dev. She bowed her head, a gentle smile gracing her lips.

"See you soon. Take care," she said.

She hurried out of the mansion, her steps light, her heart filled with an anticipation that was both exhilarating and terrifying.

Dev watched Sasi's departure, his face a mixture of admiration and worry.

"Dear," he said, his voice filled with a deep emotion that Kira hadn't heard in years. "Sasi, she's something."

"What, dear?" Kira asked, a questioning look on her face. "What are you saying?"

"Yes, dear," Dev continued, his gaze fixed on the doorway where Sasi had disappeared. "I feel she's different. And I feel that she's not only lucky for our son, but for us too. She's like a thread that holds us together, joins us, and even unites our family."

Kira, her eyes filled with a mixture of understanding and a touch of awe, looked at her husband.

"You're right, dear," she said, a gentle smile gracing her lips.

"Dear," Dev continued, his voice dropping to a softer tone, "Have you forgotten what today is?"

"What is it?" Kira asked, her mind racing, trying to recall.

"Today is the day, twenty-five years ago," Dev said, his eyes filled with a warm nostalgia, "that we first met. At the amusement park."

"Oh, yes," Kira said, a sudden rush of memories flooding her mind. "I remember. It was so coincidental, so beautiful."

Kira paused, her eyes gazing into the distance, her thoughts drifting back to that fateful day.

"What are you thinking?" Dev asked, his voice gentle.

"Nothing," Kira said, a wry smile playing on her lips. "I was just thinking what would have happened if I had never met you that day. We wouldn't have seen each other, wouldn't have fallen in love, wouldn't have gotten married, right?" She laughed, the sound light and carefree.

"Yeah, yeah," Dev said, his laughter echoing hers. "I wonder what would have happened if we hadn't met. I can't even imagine it."

They hugged, their bodies a testament to their enduring love, a love that had weathered the storms of time, a love that had become the bedrock of their family.

# THE VORTEX OF TIME

Sasi, her mind reeling, her body trembling, stood in the heart of the swirling vortex of time. The air crackled with an energy that seemed to vibrate with a primal force, a symphony of chaos and uncertainty. She had activated the Nexus watch, a watch designed to bend time to her will, and now she was caught in its maelstrom, a tiny, fragile human adrift in a sea of swirling possibilities.

Her eyes, wide with a mixture of fear and awe, scanned the vortex, its shimmering colors a kaleidoscope of light and darkness. Her heart pounded against her ribs, her breath coming in ragged gasps.

She closed her eyes, her hands instinctively shielding her face from the blinding light.

Then, silence.

She opened her eyes, her vision slowly adjusting to the darkness. The world around her was a blur of movement, a kaleidoscope of flashing lights and swirling colors. She could hear the distant hum of music, the laughter of children, the murmur of voices.

She was no longer in the lab. She was in an amusement park, the air alive with the scent of cotton candy and popcorn, the sound of joyous screams echoing through the night.

Her body ached. She had been teleported, thrown into this strange, new world, her head throbbing with the jarring transition.

She stumbled to her feet, her legs shaky, her movements clumsy.

"What happened? Where am I?" She looked around, her voice a whisper in the bustling crowd. "Rox, are you there? Please reply."

"Sasi," Rox's synthesized voice responded, its tones filled with a mixture of concern and confusion. "What happened a few minutes ago?"

"I don't know," Sasi said, her voice trembling. "I accidentally activated the watch, and then... everything is strange."

"Sasi, where is the watch? Do you have it on your hand?"

Sasi frantically searched her wrists, her fingers tracing the empty space where the watch should have been.

"I think I lost it," she whispered, her voice filled with a sense of panic. "What should I do? Oh my God, no."

"Oh, God," Rox said, its voice laced with a hint of despair. "Now we have a problem."

"First, we need to figure out where we are," Sasi said, her voice a shaky whisper.

"Yeah, right. Let me scan," Rox said, its voice filled with a sense of purpose.

But Rox's technology seemed to be malfunctioning. The scans were distorted, the information incomplete.

"What's happening, Rox?" Sasi asked, her voice laced with a growing sense of anxiety.

"Sorry, Sasi," Rox said, its voice a little apologetic. "My tech isn't working properly. It's getting a poor connection. But I'm trying my best."

Rox, with a burst of static, displayed the location and time information on a holographic screen.

Sasi stared at the details, her eyes widening in disbelief.

"Oh, no," she whispered. "How did this happen? The time..."

"What's the problem, Sasi?" Rox asked, its voice filled with a growing sense of urgency.

"Rox," Sasi said, her voice trembling, "I think the watch brought us to the past. Twenty-five years in the past. Look at the details. It says 2025."

"Oh, dear," Rox said, its voice laced with a sense of dread. "Now that's a real problem."

"Okay," Sasi said, her voice filled with a new determination. "We need to find the watch. We have to get back to our timeline."

"Yeah, Sasi," Rox said, its voice filled with a cautious optimism. "But remember, we're in the past, so let's not do anything that could change the timeline of the future, okay?"

"Okay," Sasi said, her voice a little shaky.

Sasi, her heart pounding in her chest, navigated the bustling crowd, her eyes scanning the ground, searching for the watch.

# CHAPTER TWELVE

# A TWIST OF FATE

Sasi, her heart pounding in her chest, navigated the bustling crowd, her eyes scanning the ground for the lost watch. Her mind raced, a whirlwind of confusion and a desperate hope for a way back to her timeline.

Suddenly, a young woman, her laughter echoing through the amusement park, dashed into her. The force of the collision sent Sasi stumbling backward, her body a blur of motion. The woman, startled, fumbled, dropping her phone and a handful of other items with a clatter onto the ground.

"Hey, what are you thinking?" the woman snapped, her voice sharp, her eyes narrowed. "Careful on your steps."

"Oh, sorry," Sasi said, her voice filled with remorse. "My mistake."

Sasi knelt, her fingers tracing the smooth surface of the futuristic phone that lay on the ground. A peculiar sensation rippled through her, a tingle that seemed to emanate from the earth beneath her fingertips. But she ignored it, her focus solely on helping the woman gather her scattered belongings.

As Sasi straightened, her eyes met the woman's. The woman's features were delicate, her eyes bright with a youthful energy that seemed to sparkle with life.

"Sorry again," Sasi said, her voice a little shaky.

"It's okay," the woman said, her voice softening, a warmth returning to her eyes. "Don't do that again, okay? You... what's your name?"

"I'm Sasi Rekha," Sasi replied, her voice a soft whisper.

"I'm Kira," the woman said, her eyes twinkling with a hint of curiosity.

Sasi's mind raced, a cold wave of realization washing over her. Kira? That was her mother-in-law's name.

She stared at the woman, a mixture of shock and disbelief etched on her face.

"Okay, bye," Kira said, her gaze shifting towards a nearby ride. "If we meet again, we can talk more. Bye."

Kira turned and walked away, leaving Sasi standing frozen in the center of the crowd. She couldn't shake the unsettling feeling that had gripped her heart.

"What's happening?" Rox's synthesized voice asked, its tones laced with confusion.

The ground shuddered, a subtle tremor that sent a shiver down Sasi's spine. The air crackled with a surge of electricity, the scent of ozone filling the air.

Sasi felt a cold shiver run down her spine. It was the same feeling she had experienced when she had activated the Nexus watch.

A nearby ride, a towering contraption of flashing lights and swirling metal, suddenly lurched, its electrical circuits sparking wildly. People screamed, a wave of panic spreading through the crowd, their faces contorted in a mixture of fear and confusion.

A lamppost, its base weakened by the surge of energy, began to sway precariously. Its metal frame, heavy and imposing, was poised to crash down upon Sasi.

"Sasi, watch out!" Rox's synthesized voice screamed, its tones filled with a desperate urgency.

Sasi, frozen with fear, could only watch as the lamppost descended. Then, a sudden burst of movement. A young man, his eyes filled with a mixture of concern and determination, rushed towards her. He pulled her into his arms, his body shielding her from the falling metal. He rolled them both to the ground, his movements quick and decisive, his body a bulwark against the impending disaster.

The lamppost crashed to the ground, its metal frame twisting and bending, a testament to the force of its impact. The ground trembled with the force of the fall.

Sasi, her heart pounding in her chest, opened her eyes, her gaze meeting the man's. He was looking at her, his face etched with concern.

She recognized him. It was Yash, her husband, but something was different. He was younger, his features smoother, his eyes filled with a youthful energy that she had never seen before.

The man reached out, his hand gently touching her arm.

"Are you okay?" he asked, his voice filled with genuine concern.

Sasi, her mind reeling, her heart filled with a mixture of confusion and a sense of Déjà vu, looked up at him, her eyes wide with a mixture of shock and wonder.

She took his hand, her fingers interlacing with his.

"Thank you," she said, her voice a whisper, her heart filled with a strange, unexpected sense of relief.

"But how did you get here?" she asked, her voice trembling slightly. "Yash?"

The man looked at her, his brow furrowed with confusion.

"Sorry," he said, his voice laced with a hint of amusement. "I'm not Yash. What are you talking about? My name is Dev. Anyways, nice to meet you. You should be more careful."

He smiled, his eyes twinkling with a mixture of warmth and concern.

A phone began to ring, breaking the spell of their moment. The man reached for it, turning his back to Sasi.

"Sorry," he said, as he answered the phone. "Yeah, I'm on my way. See you soon."

Sasi, her mind reeling, her heart pounding, stared at the man, her eyes filled with a mixture of disbelief and a growing sense of dread.

"Oh, dear," Rox's synthesized voice whispered, its tone filled with a chilling certainty. "I think we're both thinking the same thing, right, Sasi?"

Sasi, without a word, turned and ran. She didn't know where she was going, didn't know what to do, but she knew she couldn't stay here, couldn't face the man who looked so much like her husband, yet who was clearly someone else.

Dev, having ended the call, turned back to find that Sasi had vanished.

"Where did that girl go?" he muttered to himself. "Hmm, okay. Let's go. It's time."

Dev turned and walked away, his gaze fixed on the distant horizon.

This scene is now more focused on showing Sasi's reaction and the immediate events rather than just telling us she was shocked.

She suddenly bumped into a girl, her body a blur of movement. The girl, taken aback by the sudden collision, dropped her phone, a sleek, futuristic device, and a handful of other items onto the ground.

"Hey, what are you thinking?" the girl said, her voice a little sharp. "Careful on your steps."

"Oh, sorry," Sasi said, her voice filled with remorse. "My mistake."

Sasi knelt down, her hands reaching for the items that had scattered across the ground. A strange feeling washed over her, a feeling that she couldn't quite place, a tingling sensation that seemed to emanate from the ground. But she ignored it, her focus on helping the girl.

She stood up, her eyes meeting the girl's.

"Sorry again," she said, her voice a little shaky.

"It's okay," the girl said, her voice regaining its friendly tone. "Don't do that again, okay? You... what's your name?"

"I'm Sasi Rekha," Sasi said, her voice a soft whisper.

"I'm Kira," the girl said, her eyes twinkling with a hint of curiosity.

Sasi's mind raced. Kira? That was her mother-in-law's name.

She stared at the girl, her face a mixture of shock and disbelief.

"Okay, bye," Kira said, her eyes shifting towards a nearby ride. "If we meet again, we can talk more. Bye."

Kira turned and walked away, leaving Sasi rooted to the spot, her mind filled with a sense of bewilderment.

"What's happening?" Rox asked, its voice laced with confusion.

The ground shuddered, the air crackled with a surge of electricity.

Sasi felt a cold shiver run down her spine. It was the same feeling she had experienced when she had activated the Nexus watch.

Suddenly, a nearby ride, a towering contraption of flashing lights and swirling metal, began to malfunction. Its electrical circuits sparked, the sound echoing through the amusement park. People screamed, a wave of panic spreading through the crowd.

A nearby lamppost, its base weakened by the surge of energy, started to sway precariously. It was about to fall, its heavy metal frame poised to crush Sasi.

"Sasi, watch out!" Rox's voice screamed, its synthesized tones filled with a desperate urgency.

Sasi, frozen with fear, could only watch as the lamppost descended. Then, a sudden burst of movement. A young man, his eyes filled with a mixture of concern and determination, rushed towards her. He pulled her into his arms, his body shielding her from the falling metal. He rolled them both to the ground, his movements quick and decisive, his body a bulwark against the impending disaster.

The lamppost crashed to the ground, its metal frame twisting and bending, a testament to the force of its impact.

Sasi, her heart pounding in her chest, opened her eyes, her gaze meeting the man's. He was looking at her, his face etched with concern.

She recognized him. It was Yash, her husband, but something was different. He was younger, his features smoother, his eyes filled with a youthful energy that she had never seen before.

The man reached out, his hand gently touching her arm.

"Are you okay?" he asked, his voice filled with a genuine concern.

Sasi, her mind reeling, her heart filled with a mixture of confusion and a sense of Déjà vu, looked up at him, her eyes wide with a mixture of shock and wonder.

She took his hand, her fingers interlacing with his.

"Thank you," she said, her voice a whisper, her heart filled with a strange, unexpected sense of relief.

"But how did you get here?" she asked. "Yash?"

The man looked at her, his brow furrowed with confusion.

"Sorry," he said, his voice laced with a hint of amusement. "I'm not Yash. What are you talking about? My name is Dev. Anyways, nice to meet you. You should be more careful."

He smiled, his eyes twinkling with a mixture of warmth and concern.

A phone began to ring, breaking the spell of their moment. The man reached for it, turning his back to Sasi.

"Sorry," he said, as he answered the phone. "Yeah, I'm on my way. See you soon."

Sasi, her mind reeling, her heart pounding, stared at the man, her eyes filled with a mixture of disbelief and a growing sense of dread.

"Oh, dear," Rox's voice whispered, its tone filled with a chilling certainty. "I think we're both thinking the same thing, right, Sasi?"

Sasi, without a word, turned and ran. She didn't know where she was going, didn't know what to do, but she knew she couldn't stay here, couldn't face the man who looked so much like her husband, yet who was clearly someone else.

Dev, having ended the call, turned back to find that Sasi had vanished.

"Where did that girl go?" he muttered to himself. "Hmm, okay. Let's go. It's time."

Dev turned and walked away, his gaze fixed on the distant horizon.

# CHAPTER THIRTEEN

# THE RIPPLE EFFECT

The night air was cool and salty, the rhythmic crash of waves against the shore a calming counterpoint to the chaos that raged within Sasi. She sat on a bench overlooking the beach in park , her hands clasped tightly around her head, her eyes fixed on the distant horizon.

"Sasi," Rox's synthesized voice said, its tones laced with concern, "what's happened? I know we've created a problem. Don't worry about that guy, Aryan. He'll die one day anyway. Why are you so worried about him?"

"Rox, it's not Aryan I'm worried about," Sasi said, her voice a strained whisper. "It's the two people we met at the amusement park. The girl, Kira, and the guy, Dev. I have a feeling they're my mother-in-law and father-in-law. And that guy, Dev, has the same face as Yash - like father and son."

"Are you sure about that, Sasi?" Rox asked, its voice a little hesitant. "I remember after you left home, Kira and Dev were talking about the day they met for the first time at the amusement park twenty-five years ago. Maybe your prediction was right. It could be that young Kira and Dev we interacted with."

Sasi was stunned. "Oh my God, what have I done?" she cried out, her voice filled with a rising panic. She stood up, her movements agitated, her eyes darting around the park.

"What happened?" Rox asked, its voice filled with a mixture of confusion and apprehension. "We didn't do anything, did we?"

"No, Rox, we did," Sasi said, her voice filled with a growing despair. "We changed the entire future."

"What? How?" Rox asked, its synthesized tones a mixture of disbelief and alarm.

"Like you said, Kira and Dev met during the time we arrived here," Sasi explained, her voice a low whisper. "Dev saved Kira when that lamp was about to fall on her while she was busy on the phone. After that, they fell in love, spent time together, and eventually got married. And then Yash was born. That was the actual timeline. But now, I've changed everything. Dev saved me instead of Kira, so now they never met. The entire timeline is messed up. If they don't fall in love and get married, then my husband, Yash, would never have been born."

"Oh, no," Rox said, its voice filled with a chilling certainty. "This is bad."

"What have I done?" Sasi cried, her voice rising in a choked scream. "What should I do now?"

She looked around, her eyes filled with a desperate urgency. She was lost, alone, and facing a future that had been irrevocably altered by her actions.

Suddenly, a figure emerged from the shadows.

"Hey, lady," the watchman said, his voice laced with a hint of annoyance. "What are you doing here at this time? Go home. It's not safe here."

Sasi, her heart pounding in her chest, walked out of the park, her movements almost automatic, her mind racing.

"Sasi," Rox's synthesized voice said, its voice calm and reassuring, "I know what situation we're facing. Let's think about it later. Now the time is up, and it's not safe to stay outside. We need shelter or a rental house to live in."

"Right, Rox. Can you search for a rental house or apartment nearby?" Sasi said, her voice filled with a glimmer of hope.

"Okay, let me find it," Rox replied.

# CHAPTER FOURTEEN

# A Shelter in the Storm

The holographic map shimmered in the air, its intricate lines guiding Sasi toward a nearby apartment complex. The address and contact information flickered in the corner of the projection, a beacon of hope amidst the swirling chaos of her life. Driven by a desperate need for shelter, Sasi quickened her pace, her footsteps echoing on the deserted street.

"This apartment is best for you," Rox's synthesized voice said, its tones laced with a quiet confidence. "It has low rent fees around here."

Sasi's hand trembled slightly as she reached for the doorbell. The door swung open, and a young woman, her face radiating a warm glow, stepped into the dim light. Sasi gasped, her breath catching in her throat.

It was Zara.

Her mother, her eyes wide with surprise, her lips parting in a silent question.

Rox's synthesized voice, a mix of surprise and amusement, chimed in, "Oh, I didn't expect this."

"Hey, girl," Zara said, her voice laced with a touch of curiosity, "What's up? What do you want?"

Sasi stared at her mother, her mind reeling. The world seemed to tilt on its axis, the familiar comfort of her mother's presence a stark contrast to the fear she had been enduring.

Sasi's voice, a barely audible whisper, struggled to form the words. "Umm, I need a room to stay in this apartment."

Zara's gaze, searching Sasi's face, held a mixture of curiosity and a touch of concern. "Oh, I see," she said, her voice measured, "The room is available. But when will you pay for it?"

Sasi's heart sank, the weight of her situation pressing down on her. "I don't have any money right now, and I don't have a job," Sasi said, her voice filled with a sense of despair.

Zara's expression shifted, her eyebrows raised, her lips parting slightly in a mix of disbelief and concern. "Oh, but you're saying you don't have money or a job, either?" Zara said, her voice laced with a hint of disbelief. "Who can I give a room to? Do you know anyone here? What about your mom and dad?"

Sasi, her voice trembling, her heart heavy, knew she couldn't tell her mother about her predicament. She couldn't reveal the secrets of her journey, the chaos she had unleashed, the dangers she had escaped.

"I understand your situation," Sasi said, her voice filled with a desperate honesty. "I don't know anyone here. And my father, he... he passed away before I was born."

Her voice trailed off, her words catching in her throat. She looked away, her face contorting, her eyes filled with a mixture of sadness and a deep sense of loneliness.

"My mom," Sasi whispered, her voice barely audible, "She doesn't stay with me now. I have no one."

Zara, her voice laced with a mixture of sympathy and regret, said, "I'm sorry, but I can't give you a room. But I have an idea. You can work with me in my supermarket. You can be the counter girl. You can earn money and pay for the room. And I will get some help and support from you. Do you accept this?"

Sasi, caught between a sense of desperation and a glimmer of hope, extended her hand towards Zara. Her fingers, trembling slightly, met Zara's.

"Oh, yes," Sasi said, her voice filled with gratitude. "It's my pleasure. Thank you so much."

Sasi, her body trembling slightly, hugged Zara, her heart filled with a mix of gratitude and a strange, inexplicable sense of longing. The warmth of her mother's embrace, a familiar comfort she had longed for, was a balm to her troubled soul.

Zara, her smile softening, didn't understand the intensity of Sasi's embrace.

"Thank you, Mom," Sasi whispered, her voice barely audible.

"What?" Zara asked, her eyes filled with confusion.

"Huh, nothing," Sasi said, her voice a little shaky, her face flushed.

After the hug, Zara said, "By the way, what's your name?"

"My name is Sasi Rekha," Sasi said, her voice a whisper.

"Nice name, Sasi," Zara said, her smile widening. "Your parents must have been very happy to give you that name."

Sasi smiled back, her eyes filled with a longing for a past that she could never reclaim.

"You can call me Zara," Zara said, her tone warm and welcoming.

"Unfortunately, all the rooms are booked except for room number 111. Are you okay with that?"

"No problem, Zara," Sasi said, her voice filled with a quiet determination.

"I mean, room number 111 has features compared to the other rooms. Are you sure?" Zara said, her voice laced with a hint of concern.

"I'm sure," Sasi said, her voice firm. "I was raised in a middle-class lifestyle, so this atmosphere isn't new to me."

"Okay, then," Zara said, handing Sasi the key.

Sasi took the key, her fingers tracing its smooth surface. She turned towards the stairs, her heart filled with a mixture of hope and a sense of foreboding. She headed towards her new room, the room that had been destined for her, the room that was now her only refuge.

Sasi stood outside the door, her hand hovering over the knob, a sense of unease washing over her.

She opened the door, stepped inside, and closed the door behind her. She went to the bedroom, its walls adorned with a simple, yet comforting décor. She sat down on the bed, her body sinking into the plush mattress.

"At finally, a shelter to stay, right Sasi?" Rox said, its voice filled with a sense of relief.

Sasi, her eyes fixed on the window, her mind racing, didn't respond.

"What's wrong, Sasi?" Rox asked, its synthesized voice filled with concern.

"Everything is getting more awkward and weird," Sasi said, her voice a low murmur. "We need to solve everything soon. I don't know what things are waiting for me."

She lay down on the bed, her body exhausted, her mind filled with a mixture of fear and uncertainty. She closed her eyes, her breaths slow and shallow, trying to find a semblance of peace in the chaos that surrounded her.

She was lost in the labyrinth of time, her journey far from over, her future uncertain.

The watch, a device meant to unlock the secrets of time, had become a weapon of destruction, a tool that had irrevocably altered the course of history.

Sasi, her heart filled with a mix of fear and determination, knew that her journey was just beginning. She had to find a way to fix the future, to reunite with her husband, to make things right.

And she knew that, no matter what, she wouldn't give up.

Rox displayed the route to a nearby apartment complex, its address and contact information clearly visible. Sasi, her steps driven by a sense of urgency, headed towards the apartment complex.

"This apartment is best for you," Rox said, its voice filled with a sense of certainty. "It has low rent fees around here."

Sasi, her heart filled with a mixture of hope and apprehension, pressed the doorbell. The door swung open, and a young woman, her face radiant with a maternal glow, emerged. Sasi gasped.

It was Zara, her mother, her eyes wide with a mixture of surprise and confusion.

"Oh, I didn't expect this," Rox said, its synthesized voice a mixture of surprise and a hint of amusement.

"Hey, girl," Zara said, her voice laced with a touch of curiosity. "What's up? What do you want?"

Sasi stared at her mother, her mind reeling, her heart pounding.

"Umm, I need a room to stay in this apartment," Sasi said, her voice a low murmur.

"Oh, I see," Zara said, her eyes scanning Sasi's features. "The room is available. But when will you pay for it?"

Sasi, her heart sinking, knew she was in a difficult situation.

"I don't have any money right now, and I don't have a job," Sasi said, her voice filled with a sense of despair.

"Oh, but you're saying you don't have money or a job, either?" Zara said, her voice laced with a hint of disbelief. "Who can I give a room to? Do you know anyone here? What about your mom and dad?"

Sasi, her voice trembling, her heart heavy, knew she couldn't tell her mother about her predicament.

"I understand your situation," Sasi said, her voice filled with a desperate honesty. "I don't know anyone here. And my father, he... he passed away before I was born."

Her voice trailed off, her words catching in her throat. Her face contorted, her eyes filled with a mixture of sadness and a deep sense of loneliness.

"My mom," Sasi whispered, her voice barely audible. "She doesn't stay with me now. I have no one."

"I'm sorry, but I can't give you a room," Zara said, her voice laced with a mixture of sympathy and regret. "But I have an idea. You can work with me in my supermarket. You can be the counter girl. You can earn money and pay for the room. And I will get some help and support from you. Do you accept this?"

Sasi, caught between a sense of desperation and a glimmer of hope, extended her hand towards Zara.

"Oh, yes," she said, her voice filled with gratitude. "It's my pleasure. Thank you so much."

Sasi shook Zara's hand, a warmth spreading through her, a sense of comfort in the midst of her turmoil. She hugged Zara, her body trembling slightly, her heart filled with a mix of gratitude and a strange, inexplicable sense of longing.

Zara, her smile softening, didn't understand the intensity of Sasi's embrace.

"Thank you, Mom," Sasi whispered, her voice barely audible.

"What?" Zara asked, her eyes filled with confusion.

"Huh, nothing," Sasi said, her voice a little shaky, her face flushed.

After the hug, Zara said, "By the way, what's your name?"

"My name is Sasi Rekha," Sasi said, her voice a whisper.

"Nice name, Sasi," Zara said, her smile widening. "Your parents must have been very happy to give you that name."

Sasi smiled back, her eyes filled with a longing for a past that she could never reclaim.

"You can call me Zara," Zara said, her tone warm and welcoming.

"Unfortunately, all the rooms are booked except for room number 111. Are you okay with that?"

"No problem, Zara," Sasi said, her voice filled with a quiet determination.

"I mean, room number 111 has features compared to the other rooms. Are you sure?" Zara said, her voice laced with a hint of concern.

"I'm sure," Sasi said, her voice firm. "I was raised in a middle-class lifestyle, so this atmosphere isn't new to me."

"Okay, then," Zara said, handing Sasi the key.

Sasi took the key, her fingers tracing its smooth surface. She turned towards the stairs, her heart filled with a mixture of hope and a sense of foreboding. She headed towards her new room, the room that had been destined for her, the room that was now her only refuge.

Sasi stood outside the door, her hand hovering over the knob, a sense of unease washing over her.

She opened the door, stepped inside, and closed the door behind her. She went to the bedroom, its walls adorned with a simple, yet comforting décor. She sat down on the bed, her body sinking into the plush mattress.

"At finally, a shelter to stay, right Sasi?" Rox said, its voice filled with a sense of relief.

Sasi, her eyes fixed on the window, her mind racing, didn't respond.

"What's wrong, Sasi?" Rox asked, its synthesized voice filled with concern.

"Everything is getting more awkward and weird," Sasi said, her voice a low murmur. "We need to solve everything soon. I don't know what things are waiting for me."

She lay down on the bed, her body exhausted, her mind filled with a mixture of fear and uncertainty. She closed her eyes, her breaths slow and shallow, trying to find a semblance of peace in the chaos that surrounded her.

She was lost in the labyrinth of time, her journey far from over, her future uncertain.

The watch, a device meant to unlock the secrets of time, had become a weapon of destruction, a tool that had irrevocably altered the course of history.

Sasi, her heart filled with a mix of fear and determination, knew that her journey was just beginning. She had to find a way to fix the future, to reunite with her husband, to make things right.

And she knew that, no matter what, she wouldn't give up.

# CHAPTER FIFTEEN

# A City Under Siege

The morning sun, a pale disc struggling through the smog, cast a hazy glow over the bustling streets. A symphony of car horns and distant sirens underscored the city's frenetic pulse. Zara, her pregnancy glow amplified by the rising sun, stood outside Sasi's room, her hand hovering over the door. Her fingers tapped a gentle rhythm against the smooth surface, a subtle indication of her mounting worry.

"Sasi, wake up. It's time for work," Zara called out, her voice a blend of warmth and a hint of urgency.

"Sasi, wake up," Rox's synthesized voice said, its tones echoing through the room, a gentle nudge to the slumbering woman.

Sasi, her eyes fluttering open, sought the familiar glow of her alarm clock, but her hand found only empty space. She sat up, her movements sluggish, her mind still reeling from the events of the previous night. The memory of the bloodstained hallway, the terrifying attack, the chilling sight of Aryan's eyes, all rushed back in a wave of panic.

"Sorry for keeping you waiting," Sasi said, her voice laced with a touch of apology as she stepped out of the room. "Shall we go?"

"It's okay," Zara said, her smile reassuring. "Let's go."

They left the apartment and hailed a taxi, its tires crunching on the city's concrete arteries. Sasi, her gaze drawn to the world outside the window, instinctively lowered the glass, allowing the fresh morning air to caress her face. She took a deep breath, a wave of relief washing over her. Her senses drank in the sweet scent of blooming jasmine, the crispness of the air, the symphony of urban sounds.

"Mmm, compared to 2050," Rox's synthesized voice said, a hint of wistfulness in its tone, "the air was so much fresher twenty-five years ago. I worry that the air in our time was mostly polluted, and the oxygen levels were low compared to now, in 2025."

Zara, her gaze fixed on Sasi, smiled. She could sense the wonder in Sasi's eyes, the awe of a woman experiencing a world she had never known.

"What happened?" Zara asked, her voice laced with gentle curiosity. "Did you never feel this air before?"

"Yeah, it's new to me," Sasi said, her smile soft and genuine. She closed her eyes, her senses reveling in the experience, the beauty of a simpler time.

Outside the taxi window, a scene unfolded. A group of men, their faces hardened by a life of violence, moved through the bustling market, their eyes scanning the crowd, their hands gripping weapons. Their movements were a stark contrast to the cheerful chatter of the vendors and shoppers around them. They demanded money, destroyed stalls, and burned goods, leaving a trail of chaos and fear in their wake.

The taxi driver, his face etched with worry, said, "Don't look at them, Miss Lady. They're very dangerous people. We can't do anything about it. They're all doing this because of him, their leader."

Zara's face contorted, a mixture of worry and disgust crossing her features. She turned her gaze away, unable to bear the sight of the brutality.

But Sasi couldn't tear her eyes away. She had a sense of foreboding, a chilling realization. These men, these ruthless mercenaries, were a part of Aryan's underworld. She had unknowingly intervened in their world, saved Aryan from certain death, and now, the consequences of her actions were cascading like a domino effect, altering the very fabric of this reality.

The taxi driver's words, his warning about the leader, echoed in Sasi's mind. She remembered the burning hospital, the chilling image of Aryan, the cold, unyielding power in his eyes, the brutal murder of the police officer.

She knew, with a horrifying certainty, that her actions, her impulsive decision to save a man destined to die, had set in motion a chain of events that would have far-reaching consequences.

The taxi arrived at the supermarket, its headlights illuminating the familiar facade. As Sasi stepped out, her heart pounding in her chest, her mind filled with a mixture of fear and a sense of responsibility, she could see a grand mansion in the distance.

It was Aryan's mansion, a fortress of power, a symbol of his dominance over the city. Its silhouette against the hazy cityscape felt menacing, a constant reminder of the danger that lurked in this reality she'd landed in.

# CHAPTER SIXTEEN

# THE PRICE OF POWER

The scene shifted, taking Sasi to the interior of the mansion. A group of men, their faces hardened by a life of violence, stood around a long, polished table. They were the city's most powerful mafia members, their lives and fortunes intertwined with the rise and fall of their leader, Aryan.

A sense of tension hung in the air, the silence punctuated by the soft click of a lighter igniting.

Aryan, his face a mask of indifference, entered the room, his steps deliberate, his presence a palpable aura of power. He took a seat at the head of the table, his eyes sweeping across the room, his gaze cold and menacing.

"What?" Aryan said, his voice laced with a chilling coldness, his eyes fixed on the mafia member who dared to speak. "Come to the point, straight."

"Mr. Aryan," the mafia member said, his voice trembling slightly, "We thought you were dead, but you're alive."

Aryan looked at him, his eyes narrowed, his lips curled into a cruel smile. He reached for his cigarette, his fingers deftly manipulating the lighter.

"So, what?" Aryan said, his voice a low, threatening rumble.

"Mr. Aryan," the mafia member continued, his voice barely a whisper. "We have discussed this already. You have a drug and weapon smuggling and dealing business, and we have a share percentage deal with all the companies in the city."

Aryan still didn't care. He closed his eyes, his expression unreadable, and inhaled deeply, the smoke curling around his face, his body radiating a sense of indifference.

"So?" Aryan said, his voice a monotone.

"Before the event," the mafia member said, his voice filled with a mixture of desperation and fear, "before the shootout, we discussed it. Every company has accepted to give us their share. But there's one company, the KT company, its CEO didn't accept the offer. We tried to threaten him, but he didn't even fear us, didn't care about it. He was beaten, and unfortunately, he died. But before he died, he gave the company to his daughter, Kira. And that girl, she gave information to the police, and she complained, which caused the shootout."

The mafia member's voice trailed off, his face etched with a mixture of worry and regret.

"If that company had accepted the offer and given us the share, we wouldn't be losing profits," the mafia member said, his voice filled with a desperate plea. "And now, every other company might drop their contact with you. No one will be afraid of you anymore. What are you going to do, Mr. Aryan?"

Aryan abruptly stopped smoking, his eyes snapping open. He stood up, his movements filled with a simmering anger. He gestured to one of his mercenaries, a hulking man standing silently in the corner of the room, to come closer.

"Mr. Aryan, what are you doing?" the mafia member asked, his eyes wide with fear.

Aryan, without a word, grabbed the mercenary, his grip firm and unwavering. He twisted the mercenary's arm behind his back, his movement swift and brutal. He pulled the mercenary's gun from its holster, the weapon cold and menacing in his hand.

Aryan pointed the gun at the mercenary's back and fired, the sound of the gunshot echoing through the room. Smoke billowed out of the barrel, filling the room with a pungent aroma.

The mercenary, his body convulsing with each gunshot, fell to the ground. Aryan, his face a mask of cold indifference, picked up his cigarette, his lips curling into a cruel smile. He placed the cigarette in the dead man's mouth.

"What are you looking at?" Aryan said, his voice laced with a chilling amusement. "Do you want to know why I killed him? Oh, let me tell you. He was a police spy. He was the informant who told the police about my location when the shootout happened. He was a traitor. I knew he was a spy, but I kept him alive because I wanted to show people what I am."

The mafia members, their faces pale, their eyes wide with fear, remained silent.

"I will deal with that girl," Aryan said, his voice a low, threatening rumble. "She'll pay for what she's done. And I'll show her hell."

Aryan's laughter, a chilling sound that echoed through the room, was laced with a mixture of malice and a sense of twisted justice.

He slammed his fists on the table, the sound reverberating through the room.

"So, do you have anything to say?" he asked, his eyes scanning the faces of the cowering mafia members.

The mafia member, his voice a trembling whisper, said, "No."

Aryan, his rage burning bright, kicked the dead mercenary's body, his movement filled with a cruel, sadistic delight.

He turned and walked towards the stairs, his steps deliberate, his presence radiating a chilling sense of power.

The remaining mercenaries dragged the dead mercenary's body away, their movements swift and efficient.

Aryan reached his room, his steps heavy, his mind consumed by the need for revenge.

The maid, a woman whose eyes reflected a lifetime of hardship and fear, entered the room.

"Sir," she said, her voice barely a whisper. "I found this in your clothes. I was washing them, and I found this watch."

She handed Aryan the watch, its silver surface glinting under the dim light of the room.

Aryan, his brow furrowed, took the watch, his eyes scanning its intricate design, his fingers tracing its smooth surface.

"How did this watch get here?" Aryan said, his voice laced with a mixture of confusion and curiosity. "Whose is it? This watch looks different."

He read the inscription on the front and back of the watch, "Nexus."

"Nexus?" Aryan muttered, his voice filled with a sense of unease. "What brand is it?"

"I don't care," Aryan said, his voice filled with a sense of defiance. "Wait, I've seen this watch before. I remember I found it on the ground at the amusement park. And then, after that, the shootout happened."

Aryan stared at the Nexus watch, his eyes narrowing, his mind racing, trying to make sense of the bizarre sequence of events. He knew that the watch was somehow connected to his survival, but he couldn't figure out how.

He slipped the watch onto his wrist, its metal band cool against his skin.

He felt a surge of power, a sense of invincibility. But a deep sense of unease lingered, a gnawing feeling that something was not right.

Aryan was a man who lived in the shadows, a man who had built his empire on violence and fear. He was accustomed to controlling the world around him, to bending the rules to his will.

But now, he was faced with something he couldn't control, something that had defied his understanding, something that had thrown his meticulously crafted world into chaos.

Aryan had always been a master of his domain, a predator at the top of the food chain. But now, he was hunted, a prey caught in the web of time, the very fabric of reality twisted and distorted by forces beyond his control.

He was a man who lived by the rules of power and violence, but now, he was faced with a power he couldn't understand, a power that could rewrite the very laws of existence.

# CHAPTER SEVENTEEN

# A HAVEN IN THE SUPERMARKET

The fluorescent lights of the supermarket cast a sterile glow over the neatly arranged aisles, a stark contrast to the vibrant, chaotic world outside. Zara, her pregnant belly a gentle bump beneath her stylish dress, watched with a mixture of pride and concern as Sasi, now clad in the supermarket's uniform, moved with a practiced ease, arranging products on the shelves.

"Sasi, you're doing great!" Zara said, her voice a blend of encouragement and a touch of amusement.

Sasi, her smile genuine, returned Zara's warmth. She had found a temporary haven in this bustling supermarket, a place where she could earn a living, a place where she could feel a sense of purpose, a place where she could, for a few moments, forget the chaos that swirled around her.

But the world she had stumbled into was far from predictable.

Suddenly, Sasi noticed a familiar figure. Dev, the man who had saved her from the falling lamppost, the man who, for a moment, had seemed to be a younger version of her husband, was browsing the aisles.

Sasi, her heart pounding in her chest, watched as Dev, his face a mixture of confusion and a sense of bewilderment, searched for a specific product. He seemed lost, his eyes scanning the shelves, his brow furrowed.

He looked up, his gaze meeting Sasi's. He gave a small, almost involuntary gasp.

"Hey," Dev said, his voice a blend of surprise and a touch of familiarity. "You... the girl from the amusement park. I can't believe I'm meeting you here. How are you? Are you working here?"

Sasi, her mind racing, her heart pounding, walked towards Dev.

"Oh, hey!" Sasi said, her voice a little shaky. "Yes."

"By the way," Dev said, his voice laced with a hint of awkwardness, "I forgot to ask you. What's your name again?"

"I'm Sasi Rekha," Sasi said, her voice a soft whisper. "You can call me Sasi."

"Sasi," Dev said, his smile genuine. "Nice name." He gave a thumbs up.

"Shall we go outside and have a cup of coffee?" Dev asked, his eyes twinkling with a mixture of curiosity and a hint of charm.

Sasi's mind raced. She knew that she couldn't let Dev fall for her. He was her father-in-law, even if he wasn't aware of it yet. And she was a married woman, a fact she had already revealed to him.

"Oh, I'm so sorry," Sasi said, her voice laced with a hint of regret. "I'm already married."

Dev's face contorted, a mixture of disappointment and surprise crossing his features.

"What? Married?" Dev said, his voice filled with disbelief. "I can't believe it. I'm sorry if I said anything wrong."

"It's okay," Sasi said, her voice a gentle murmur. "We can still be friends."

"This is the only way I can keep in touch with him," Sasi thought, her mind racing, her inner voice a quiet whisper.

Sasi extended her hand, offering a handshake. Dev, his initial disappointment fading, reached out and shook her hand. They became friends.

Zara, her eyes sharp and observant, walked towards them.

"Sasi, where are you going?" Zara said, her voice a mixture of concern and a touch of urgency. "It's urgent."

Sasi, her heart pounding, turned towards Zara.

"Sasi, guide that guy," Zara said, her finger pointing towards a man standing by the cash register.

Sasi looked at the man, her eyes widening in disbelief.

"Who is he?" Sasi asked, her voice filled with a sense of confusion.

"He's the manager of the KT company. It's owned by Kira, that woman," Zara said.

Sasi's mind raced, her memories flickering.

"What? Kira?" Sasi whispered, her voice filled with a sudden sense of understanding. "I remember now. Kira and Dev... They were talking about this KT company. And later, Dev became the CEO of the company."

"Sasi, are you listening?" Zara said, her voice laced with a hint of impatience.

"Yes," Sasi said, her voice a little shaky.

"Guide him, help him take the products to the company. He's going there right now," Zara said.

Sasi, her heart filled with a mixture of trepidation and a sense of purpose, went to help the manager.

She knew this was a chance, a chance to see both Kira and Dev again. She had to get them together. She had to set things right.

Suddenly, a box, its contents heavy and unwieldy, fell off the shelf, its trajectory aimed directly at Sasi's head.

Dev, his reflexes as sharp as his wit, grabbed the box, his hand catching it just in time.

"Thanks, Dev," Sasi said, her voice filled with a mixture of gratitude and relief.

"No mention," Dev said, his smile warm and genuine.

He noticed Sasi struggling to move the heavy box.

"Wait, let me help you," Dev said, his voice filled with a sense of chivalry.

Dev took half of the luggage, his arms strong and steady.

After the manager paid for the products, Dev and Sasi carried the luggage to the manager's car.

"Thanks," the manager said, his voice laced with a sense of gratitude. "Can you do me another favor? My helpers aren't available today. Can you come with me and help me arrange this luggage in the office?"

Sasi's heart pounded, her mind racing. She could use this as an opportunity to see Kira and Dev again.

"Oh, yes," Sasi said, her voice filled with a newfound confidence. "Wait, I'll call someone to help."

"Okay," the manager said, his gaze shifting to Dev.

Dev, his face filled with a mixture of curiosity and a hint of anticipation, stood by the car, waiting for Sasi.

"Dev, wait," Sasi said, her voice filled with a sense of urgency. "Can you come with me to KT Company and help?"

Dev hesitated, his brow furrowed with a mixture of hesitation and a flicker of desire.

"Okay, let's go," Dev said, his voice laced with a hint of excitement. "Since I was a kid, I've been thinking about entering KT Company. I even applied for a job there, but they rejected me. So at least now, I can enter the company with you." He smiled, his eyes sparkling with a sense of playful mischief.

Sasi and Dev, along with the manager, climbed into the car.

# CHAPTER EIGHTEEN

# A TANGLED WEB

The drive to the KT company was short, but it felt like a journey through time. The exterior of the company, a towering skyscraper of glass and steel, exuded a sense of power and ambition.

They reached the parking lot, and the manager asked them to carry the boxes to the top floor. He then left, his movements hurried, his eyes fixed on his destination.

Dev and Sasi carried the luggage, the weight of the boxes heavy on their shoulders.

"What's the final floor?" Dev asked, his voice laced with a hint of disbelief. "This guy is serious. He's not joking, is he?"

Sasi looked at Dev, her eyes filled with a mixture of apprehension and a sense of urgency.

"Yeah, it's a tough climb to the final floor with this luggage," Sasi said, her voice a whisper. "Let's go, Dev."

They entered the elevator, the doors closing behind them, isolating them from the world outside.

They felt the elevator ascend, the sensation of the journey a subtle reminder of their precarious position.

As the elevator doors closed, a group of mercenaries, their faces etched with a chilling intensity, entered the building. They moved with a practiced precision, their eyes scanning the halls, their hands gripping weapons. They had come for a purpose.

They blocked the main gate, their presence a chilling reminder of the power that lay behind the company's gleaming facade. They then locked the parking area, ensuring that no one could escape. Finally, they stormed towards the stairs, their footsteps echoing through the building.

On the top floor, in a spacious boardroom, Kira, dressed in a stylish office suit, sat at a mahogany table, her gaze fixed on the man across from her.

"Let's come to the point, straight, Ms. Kira," the mafia member said, his voice laced with a chilling threat. "Let's finish this up. You give us your share of the company. Or you'll suffer. Our boss was ready to destroy you. If you want to live, sign this contract. Next time, we won't come here. If Mr. Aryan comes, the discussion will be brutal. Think about it, Ms. Kira. Sign the contract and hand over the company share. It's not a request, it's a warning."

Kira, her eyes blazing with fury, picked up the contract, its pages crisp and official. She tossed the document across the table, landing squarely on the mafia member's face.

"Just get out of my company," Kira said, her voice a mixture of rage and defiance. "I won't do any contract with you guys. I'm not afraid of you or your boss, Aryan. Do whatever you can. Now, get lost from my company."

"You'll face the consequences, Ms. Kira," the mafia member said, his voice laced with a chilling threat. "It's too late. We've already taken control of this building. My men are surrounding your company."

Kira, her face pale, her heart pounding, realized the gravity of the situation. She stood up, her movements a mixture of fear and determination, and rushed out of the boardroom.

She reached the hallway, her steps quick and determined. But the mercenaries, their forms a menacing barricade, blocked her exit.

Just then, Dev and Sasi arrived on the top floor, their arms burdened by the heavy luggage. Sasi, her eyes widening in horror, saw Kira surrounded by the mercenaries.

"Oh, no!" Sasi cried, her voice filled with a desperate urgency. "Kira is in danger!"

Dev, his face a mixture of confusion and a hint of concern, stared at the scene unfolding before him.

Sasi, her mind racing, had a sudden idea.

"Dev," Sasi said, her voice filled with a sense of urgency. "Go. Go and save her."

"What?" Dev said, his eyes widening in disbelief. "Save her? Why? Why should I fight with them?"

"Just go," Sasi said, her voice a mixture of desperation and a sense of conviction.

She shoved Dev towards Kira and the mercenaries.

Dev stumbled forward, his movements awkward and uncertain. He collided with Kira, their bodies crashing to the ground.

They looked at each other, their eyes meeting, a silent acknowledgment of their shared predicament.

Dev, his face now a mask of determination, stood up. Kira, her eyes filled with a mixture of fear and a sense of disbelief, followed suit.

"Hey, who are you?" one of the mercenaries said, his voice laced with a mocking tone. "Just go away. It's not your problem."

Dev tried to respond, but another mercenary cut him off.

"Hey, guys, look," the second mercenary said, his voice laced with a mocking laugh. "This kid thinks he's a hero."

The mercenaries began to push and shove Dev, their movements filled with a sense of amusement, their taunts echoing through the hall.

"Did you think you were a hero?" one of the mercenaries said, his laughter echoing through the hall. "Show us, Mr. Hero. Save the girl from us, you little hero."

Sasi, her heart pounding in her chest, watched with a mixture of terror and hope. She knew Dev was not a hero. But in this moment, she had no choice but to believe.

She whistled, a shrill sound that echoed through the hall, her voice filled with a mixture of urgency and encouragement. "Go for it, Dev!"

All the mercenaries surrounded Dev, their expressions a blend of amusement and menace.

Dev, his anger boiling over, grabbed the mercenary closest to him, twisting his arm behind his back with a sharp, powerful movement. He then broke the mercenary's arm, the sound of bone cracking a chilling testament to his strength.

He then pulled the mercenary close, his gaze fixed on the man's face, and delivered a swift, powerful kick to the man's chest, sending the mercenary crashing to the floor.

The other mercenaries, their initial amusement replaced by a sense of shock and fear, backed away.

Sasi, her eyes wide with a mixture of disbelief and admiration, cheered, her voice a mixture of excitement and encouragement.

"Go, Dev, go!"

The mercenaries, their sense of superiority shattered, moved to surround Dev.

Dev, his anger fueling his movements, fought back with a ferocity that surprised even himself. He moved with a grace that belied his lack of training, his body a blur of motion.

He blocked, he dodged, he countered, his punches precise and powerful, his kicks swift and lethal.

Kira, her gaze fixed on Dev, her eyes filled with a mixture of disbelief and a sense of awe, couldn't help but be impressed by his fighting prowess.

One by one, the mercenaries fell, their bodies crashing to the ground, their expressions a mixture of pain and shock.

A wave of adrenaline coursed through Dev, his movements faster, his determination even stronger.

He confronted the leader of the mercenaries, a hulking man with a face that seemed to have been carved out of granite.

The mercenary leader, his eyes burning with a cold fury, charged towards Dev, his arms swinging, his movements a blur of violence.

Dev, his body a whirlwind of motion, managed to dodge the mercenary's attack.

He then grabbed the mercenary's arm, twisting it with a powerful movement. He then kicked the mercenary, a swift, devastating blow that sent the man crashing to the ground.

Dev, his anger fueling his every move, grabbed the mercenary's arm and twisted it, breaking his elbow with a sickening crunch. Then, with a powerful kick, he dislocated the mercenary's shoulder. The mercenary, his face contorted in agony, fell to the ground, his movements a desperate struggle for air.

The mercenaries, their leader incapacitated, turned and fled, their retreat a chaotic scramble, a desperate attempt to escape the wrath of a man they had underestimated.

The mercenaries removed the blockade they had created, the gate swinging open, the parking area accessible once again. They carried their leader away, their faces a mixture of defeat and fear.

Sasi, her breath catching in her throat, watched as the mercenaries disappeared.

She turned to Dev, a sense of gratitude and awe filling her heart. She had witnessed his courage, his strength, his resilience. He had saved her mother-in-law, the woman she was destined to call her mother.

She had a feeling, a sense of certainty, that this encounter, this moment of unexpected heroism, was going to change everything.

Sasi waited for Kira to say something, to acknowledge Dev's bravery, to express her gratitude. But Kira, her expression unreadable, turned and walked away, her movements swift and determined.

Sasi's heart sank.

"What?" Dev said, his voice a mixture of annoyance and disbelief. "Not even a thanks, huh? You've got that much ego? Fine, I'm done with her." He turned to Sasi, his face filled with a mixture of anger and a hint of amusement.

"Okay, Sasi, let's go arrange the luggage and get out of this company," Dev said. "I used to like this company. I dreamed of working here. But the CEO, she's a devil. An ego queen. Come on, let's go."

Dev, his anger still simmering, dragged Sasi towards the luggage, his movements filled with a sense of frustration. They carried the luggage outside, their steps heavy with a sense of disappointment.

"Okay, Sasi," Dev said, his smile a little strained, "See you tomorrow. Bye. Can you make it home okay?"

"Yes," Sasi said, her voice a soft whisper. "Thanks, Dev."

"Hey, no need to say thanks," Dev said, his smile returning. "At least you're not as rude as that CEO. What was her name again? Kira, right? I'm done with her."

Dev turned and walked away, his footsteps echoing through the parking lot, his mind filled with a mixture of anger and a sense of disappointment.

Sasi, her heart heavy with a mix of confusion and a sense of hope, watched him leave.

A taxi pulled up, its engine purring softly. Sasi climbed in, her mind filled with a whirlwind of thoughts.

"Oh, Sasi," Rox said, its synthesized voice filled with a sense of concern, "Everything is happening so weird. Kira and Dev met. But they hate each other now. What a headache. How are you going to solve this?"

"I'll figure it out, Rox," Sasi said, her voice a firm whisper.

The taxi driver, a man whose face bore the lines of a life lived in the city, looked at Sasi, his eyes filled with a mixture of curiosity and concern.

"Madam, who are you talking to? Whose voice is that?" he asked, his voice laced with a hint of apprehension.

"Huh, no," Sasi said, her voice a little shaky. "Never mind. It's just a phone call."

"Oh, okay, Madam," the taxi driver said, his voice filled with a sense of resignation.

The sun dipped below the horizon, casting a golden glow over the city. The taxi pulled up to Sasi's apartment.

Sasi stepped out of the taxi, her body exhausted, her mind filled with a mixture of fatigue and a sense of urgency.

Zara, her eyes filled with a mixture of worry and concern, approached Sasi.

"Hey, Sasi, where have you been all this time?" Zara asked, her voice laced with a hint of impatience.

"I was just working," Sasi said, her voice a little strained. "I helped that manager, and I arranged the luggage in the office. I'm tired and I have a headache. I need to rest."

"Yes, yes, I know you've done your job," Zara said, her voice filled with reassurance. "I was just worried because you weren't back in time. That's why."

"Okay, Zara," Sasi said, her voice a gentle murmur. "Good night."

"Good night, dear," Zara said, her voice soft and warm.

Zara, her heart filled with a mixture of confusion and concern, watched as Sasi entered her apartment.

"I don't know why I feel so familiar with her," Zara thought, her mind filled with a strange sense of connection. "I feel so sad when she's upset. I worry about her more than I should. I don't know why. But anyway, she's a good girl."

Zara smiled, her eyes fixed on the door, her heart filled with a mother's love, a love that transcended the boundaries of time and the twists of fate.

She turned and walked towards her own room, her steps slow, her mind filled with a sense of foreboding. She knew that Sasi had stumbled into a dangerous world, a world of secrets, of hidden truths, of a past that had come to haunt the future.

But Zara knew that, no matter what, she would be there for Sasi, a beacon of love and support in a world filled with shadows and uncertainty.

# THE ECHOES OF CHAOS

The fluorescent lights of the supermarket buzzed overhead, casting a sterile glow over the neatly arranged aisles. Sasi, her movements a blur of practiced efficiency, restocked the shelves with shampoo and conditioner bottles. She was a whirlwind of action, but her mind was a storm of its own. The chaos she'd unleashed, the ripple effect of her actions, hung over her like a dark cloud. This world, a world she'd stumbled into, felt more and more like a labyrinth of shadows, where danger lurked in every corner.

Zara, her face pale and her hand pressed against her forehead, turned to Sasi.

"Sasi," Zara said, her voice laced with concern, "Take care of the shop. I have a headache. I'm going home. You come home tonight, okay?"

"Zara..." Sasi began, her voice filled with a mix of worry and a longing to stay by her mother's side. "Why are you staying? Let me come with you."

"No, I'm fine," Zara said, her smile forced, her eyes reflecting a weariness that Sasi couldn't ignore. "I can take care of myself."

Zara turned and hurried out of the store, her steps quick, a silhouette of worry against the bright lights of the supermarket.

Moments later, a figure stumbled into the supermarket, his body a testament to violence. He was covered in blood, a large knife protruding from his back, his face contorted in pain. His eyes, wide with fear and desperation, scanned the crowd.

"Please, someone help me," he gasped, his voice a ragged whisper. He reached out, his hand trembling, pleading for mercy.

A group of mercenaries, their faces hard, their eyes cold, their hands gripping bloodied blades, surged forward. They surrounded the wounded man, their movements swift and brutal, a terrifying symphony of death. Their blades flashed in the fluorescent light, a chilling reflection of their grim purpose.

The patrons of the supermarket, their faces frozen in terror, hurried towards the back of the store, their movements a scramble for safety.

Sasi, her heart pounding in her chest, found herself rooted in place, paralyzed by the horror unfolding before her. Her eyes met the wounded man's, and a wave of recognition washed over her.

"This is the manager from KT Company," Sasi thought, her mind reeling, her heart pounding with a horrifying sense of Déjà vu. "He was the one who took me and Dev to the company. What happened to him? Why are they attacking him?"

She stared at the manager, her body numb, her mind paralyzed with a sense of helplessness. Her hand instinctively flew to her mouth, as if to stifle a scream.

"What should I do?" Sasi thought, her voice a silent whisper, a desperate plea in the face of unimaginable violence. "I can't do anything. It's my fault. Because of me, he's suffering."

A sleek, black car pulled up outside the store. The engine roared, a jarring sound in the sudden silence. Aryan emerged from the car, his face a mask of cold fury, his body radiating a chilling sense of power. He was covered in blood, his eyes burning with a cold, unyielding intensity.

He entered the store, his footsteps echoing on the tiled floor, his presence a palpable force of darkness. The mercenaries, their blades dripping with blood, hurried towards Aryan, offering their weapons to their leader.

Aryan took the bloodied blade, its metal surface reflecting the harsh fluorescent lights. He approached the manager, his movements slow and deliberate. He grabbed the manager's shirt, his fingers digging into the man's flesh, his gaze a chilling blend of malice and a cruel, twisted amusement. A thin, cruel smile curled his lips.

"Oh, you don't know what you've done?" Aryan said, his voice a chilling rasp, his smile an icy mockery. "I need information about two people. A girl, and a man. Especially the guy who beat and touched my men."

Aryan's rage, a boiling cauldron of fury, bubbled over. He slammed his hand on the counter, the sound echoing through the store.

"I need him," Aryan said, his voice filled with a chilling intensity. "How dare he touch my men? And he saved Kira! And there was a girl with him. They both destroyed my plan. They both interfered with my plans. They will pay for what they've done."

"I don't know them," the manager said, his voice a desperate plea. "I didn't do anything to your men. What have I done?"

Aryan, his anger reaching a fever pitch, shoved the manager to the ground, his movements a terrifying display of raw power. Aryan stood there, his face contorted with rage, his eyes burning with a cold, unyielding fury.

He reached for the blade, its metal surface cold and menacing in his hand.

"So, you're saying you didn't do anything?" Aryan said, his voice dripping with sarcasm.

"You're the one who brought them to the company, from here," Aryan said, his voice a low, threatening growl. "Now show me who that person is. I know that girl works here. Show me."

The manager, his body wracked with pain, his eyes filled with a desperate fear, tried to raise his hand, to point towards Sasi, but he was unable to hold himself up. He crumpled to the ground, his body a silent testament to the brutal violence he had endured.

Aryan, his patience wearing thin, his anger reaching its peak, shook his head.

"Okay, you're done," Aryan said, his voice laced with a chilling finality. "I'm done with you."

Aryan, his movements swift and brutal, raised the blade, its sharp edge glinting under the fluorescent lights, and brought it down on the manager's neck. The sound of the blade slicing through flesh was a sickening, chilling sound. The air hung heavy with the scent of blood.

The manager, his eyes wide with a mixture of horror and disbelief, collapsed to the ground, his body a lifeless heap.

The patrons in the store, their faces frozen in terror, screamed, their cries a symphony of fear and a desperate scramble for safety. The people in the store surged towards the exits, a panicked mass of humanity.

The blood, thick and red, spilled across the floor, staining the once-sterile environment. Aryan's clothes and face were spattered with blood, a chilling testament to the savagery of his act. He stared at the blood, a chilling gleam in his eyes.

Aryan, his face contorted with rage, his eyes burning with a cold, unyielding fury, raised the blade high above his head. His voice echoed through the store, a chilling declaration of revenge.

"I'll find them and I'll make them pay for what they've done!"

Sasi, her heart pounding in her chest, her body trembling with fear, watched from the doorway. She had become a target, a victim of the chaos she had unwittingly unleashed.

"Sasi, we need to leave," Rox's synthesized voice said, its tones laced with a sense of urgency. "Come on."

Sasi, her mind racing, her senses heightened, noticed something. She looked closer, her eyes fixed on Aryan's waist. She saw it. The Nexus watch, its silver surface gleaming under the fluorescent lights.

"Oh, shit," Rox said, its voice filled with a sense of dread. "How is this possible? How did Aryan get that watch? Sasi, we have another problem."

Sasi, her mind reeling, stood frozen in place, her eyes wide with disbelief.

She had saved Aryan from death, had unintentionally set in motion a chain of events that had led to the manager's death. And now, Aryan had the watch, the Nexus watch, the very watch that had brought her to this time, this world.

"What have I done?" Sasi thought, her voice a silent whisper, her mind consumed by a sense of guilt and a growing sense of fear. "I thought Kira was the only one in danger. But now, I've intentionally involved Dev in this. And myself. What am I going to do?"

Sasi, her fear turning to panic, began to frantically pull at her hair, her fingers digging into her scalp, her body wracked with a wave of despair. She screamed, her cries echoing through the store, a testament to the terror that had gripped her heart.

A taxi, its engine humming, pulled up outside the store. Sasi hurried towards the car, her movements frantic.

She threw herself into the car, her body shaking with a mixture of fear and a desperate need to escape.

"What have I done?" Sasi thought, her mind racing, her voice a frantic whisper. "I'm so scared."

# THE UNMASKING OF TRUTH

Then Sasi arrived at her apartment. Sasi stood at the threshold of Zara's room, a wave of apprehension washing over her. She had been filled with a sense of urgency, a desperate need to tell Zara about the horrifying events at the supermarket, but now, as she looked at the bloodstains that marred the hallway floor, a cold dread settled in her heart.

"Zara, may I come in?" Sasi asked, her voice a soft whisper, her words barely audible over the pounding of her heart.

Sasi carefully entered the room, her eyes scanning the space, her gaze following the trail of blood that led to the bedroom.

She hurried towards the bedroom, her steps quick and purposeful. She slammed the door shut behind her, the sound echoing in the quiet apartment.

Zara lay on the floor, her face pale, her eyes closed, her body limp. A thin trickle of blood stained her lips.

"Mom," Sasi cried out, her voice a mix of fear and a desperate plea. "No!"

She rushed to Zara's side, her hands reaching out to lift her. With a gentle strength, she lifted Zara and carried her to the bed. She laid her down gently, her fingers tracing Zara's cheek, her heart pounding in her chest.

She tried to wake Zara, but her mother remained unresponsive.

"Oh, God, what do I do?" Sasi whispered, her voice filled with a desperate panic.

She grabbed a glass of water from the bedside table and splashed it onto Zara's face.

Zara's eyes fluttered open, her gaze meeting Sasi's.

"Oh, Sasi, thank you for saving me," Zara said, her voice a mixture of relief and gratitude. "You came at the right time."

"Zara, what happened?" Sasi asked, her voice filled with a desperate need to understand. "Are you okay?"

Zara, her breathing still ragged, her movements slow, sat up in bed.

"Nothing, Sasi," Zara said, her voice a little shaky. "It's just normal pain. That's it."

"But why did you come here?" Zara asked, her voice filled with a mixture of curiosity and concern. "I told you to take care of the store. What brought you here?"

Sasi, her mind racing, her heart pounding, struggled to find the words to explain the terrifying events she had witnessed.

"I came here to tell you something," Sasi said, her voice a mixture of urgency and a hint of fear.

Sasi started to describe the events at the supermarket. She told Zara about the brutal murder of the manager, the chilling appearance of Aryan, the cold, ruthless rage in his eyes. She described the terrifying scene, the chaos, the bloodshed, the sense of fear that had gripped her heart.

Zara, her face a mixture of disbelief, horror, and a sense of guilt, listened in stunned silence. Her hands trembled, her eyes darted around the room, and her breathing became shallow.

"Wait, Zara," Sasi said, her voice filled with a sense of urgency. "I think you're hiding something from me. Tell me. Now."

Zara, her movements slow and deliberate, got out of bed. She opened a drawer in her bedside table and pulled out a photograph.

"This is my husband," Zara said, her voice a low murmur, her eyes filled with a mixture of sadness and regret. "And the father of my child."

She gently touched her pregnant belly, her fingers tracing the curve of her stomach.

Sasi, her heart pounding, her mind reeling, took the photograph from Zara's hand.

She slowly flipped the photograph over, her eyes widening in disbelief. Aryan, his face a mask of arrogance and ruthlessness, stood beside Zara, their arms wrapped around each other. They were a couple, a seemingly normal couple, captured in a moment of intimacy.

Sasi stared at the photo, her hands trembling, her mind struggling to grasp the impossible truth.

"Oh, my God, I didn't expect this twist," Rox said, its synthesized voice filled with a sense of disbelief.

Sasi looked at the photo, her mind racing, her heart pounding.

"Then... is Aryan my father?" she whispered, her voice filled with a mixture of shock and disbelief.

Aryan, the man who had terrorized the city, the man who had threatened her life, the man who had killed the manager, was her father.

The truth, a chilling, unthinkable revelation, had shattered her world.

She remembered the Nexus watch, the watch that Aryan had worn. She remembered Zara's hesitation, her reluctance to answer her questions, her desperation to protect her.

She remembered the day she had arrived in 2025, the moment she had stumbled into this world, and the feeling of familiarity that had swept over her.

She had always felt a connection to Zara, an unspoken bond that transcended the boundaries of logic and reason.

And now, she understood.

She was Aryan's daughter. And he was her father.

# CHAPTER TWENTY-ONE

# UNVEILING THE PAST

Aryan, the man who had terrorized the city, the man who had threatened her life, the man who had killed the manager, was her father.

The truth, a chilling, unthinkable revelation, had shattered Sasi's world.

She remembered the Nexus watch, the watch that Aryan had worn. She remembered Zara's hesitation, her reluctance to answer her questions, her desperation to protect her.

She remembered the day she had arrived in 2025, the moment she had stumbled into this world, and the feeling of familiarity that had swept over her.

She had always felt a connection to Zara, an unspoken bond that transcended the boundaries of logic and reason.

And now, she understood.

She was Aryan's daughter. And he was her father.

Sasi's mind raced, trying to piece together the fragments of her past. She remembered her mother's words, her whispers of a father who had been gone before she was even born. She remembered the emptiness, the void that had always been at the center of her life.

And now, she understood the source of that void. Her father had been a criminal, a man who had built his empire on violence and fear.

She looked at Zara, her mother, her eyes filled with a mixture of confusion and a growing sense of understanding.

Zara, her face etched with a mix of sadness and a quiet strength, looked at Sasi, her eyes filled with a depth of emotion that Sasi had never seen before.

"I left him," Zara said, her voice a low whisper, her eyes filled with a mixture of pain and resignation. "I took over the grocery store, turned it into a supermarket. Aryan became a rich man, a most wanted criminal. A few months later, I decided to kill myself."

Zara paused, her gaze fixed on the floor, her voice filled with a raw, unvarnished honesty.

"But then, I found out I was pregnant," Zara continued, her voice trembling slightly, her hand gently caressing her stomach. "And I started living for my baby."

"He never stopped looking for me," Zara said, her voice laced with a hint of bitterness. "He thought I would come back to him. But I never would."

Zara, her eyes welling up, reached for a tissue and wiped away her tears.

Sasi, her heart filled with a mixture of sympathy and a sense of overwhelming sadness, stood up and wrapped her arms around Zara. She held her mother tightly, her embrace filled with a sense of comfort and support.

"Don't worry, Mom," Sasi whispered, her voice filled with a gentle reassurance.

Rox, its synthesized voice a soft, gentle whisper, said, "Oops, Sasi!"

Zara, her eyes widening in surprise, looked at Sasi, her face filled with a mixture of confusion and alarm.

"What?" Zara asked, her voice filled with a sense of bewilderment. "Mom?"

Zara, her voice a mixture of surprise and a touch of fear, turned to Sasi, her eyes filled with a mixture of confusion and a desperate need to understand.

"Sasi, what are you saying?" Zara asked, her voice laced with a sense of urgency. "Do you have something on your mind?"

Sasi, her eyes filled with a mixture of sadness and a sense of determination, told her mother everything. She recounted her arrival in 2025, her meeting with Yash, the discovery of the Nexus watch, her encounters with Kira and Dev, the devastating consequences of altering the timeline, and the terrifying events at the supermarket.

Zara, her face a mask of disbelief, stood there, her mind reeling.

"I can't believe this," Zara said, her voice a soft whisper. "Are you saying it's true?"

"I know it's hard to believe," Sasi said, her voice filled with a mixture of desperation and a sense of urgency. "But I have no choice, Mom."

Zara, her eyes filled with a mixture of sympathy and a sense of overwhelming sadness, reached out and touched Sasi's face, her fingers gently caressing her daughter's cheek.

"Don't worry, dear," Zara said, her voice filled with a comforting reassurance. "I don't know if you're telling the truth or not, but I'll help you. I'll be here to support you, my sweetheart, Sasi."

Sasi, her heart filled with a mixture of gratitude and a sense of overwhelming relief, leaned into her mother's embrace.

"I love you, Mom," Sasi whispered, her voice filled with tears, her words echoing her love, her gratitude, her despair.

Zara, her eyes filled with tears, kissed Sasi's forehead, her touch a testament to the unbreakable bond of mother and daughter.

Sasi, her heart filled with a mixture of fear and a sense of hope, knew that her journey was far from over. She had stumbled into a world of secrets, a world of danger, a world where the lines between past, present, and future were blurred, a world where the consequences of her actions, her choices, her mistakes, were far-reaching, unpredictable, and devastating.

But she also knew that she was not alone. She had her mother, her love, her support. And she had Rox, her faithful AI companion, her guide through this chaotic labyrinth.

She knew that she had to find a way to fix the future, to make things right, to find her way back to her husband, to Yash.

And she knew that, no matter what challenges lay ahead, she wouldn't give up. She would fight, she would persevere, she would find her way back to the life she had lost.

# CHAPTER TWENTY-TWO

# PARTY OF LOVE

then next day ,The city lights, a dazzling constellation of neon and glass, painted the night in vibrant hues. The air buzzed with energy, a symphony of laughter, music, and the intoxicating rhythm of a city that never slept.

Sasi, her phone clutched in her hand, listened to the voice on the other end of the line.

"Hey, Sasi, it's me, Dev," the voice said, a mixture of warmth and a touch of hesitant charm in its tone.

"Dev? Hey, how are you?" Sasi responded, her voice laced with a hint of surprise. "How did you get my number?"

"I found it," Dev said, his voice dropping to a conspiratorial whisper. "Never mind that now... So, what's up?"

"What's the matter, Dev?" Sasi asked, her mind racing.

"Actually, I got some tickets for the best, most popular party club in the city," Dev said, his voice tinged with a playful excitement. "So, shall we go? It's up to you, Sasi!"

Sasi hesitated. She was still reeling from the events of the past few days, her mind consumed by the complexities of her situation. But a part of her, a small, rebellious part, craved a distraction, a moment of escape.

"Okay, Dev," Sasi said, her voice a mixture of resignation and a touch of excitement. "Send me the location."

"Rox," Sasi whispered, her eyes searching for the AI companion. "Show me the route."

Rox, ever helpful, displayed the route to the club on a holographic screen, the directions flashing in vivid detail.

"Hey, Sasi, you're going to a party," Rox said, its voice a gentle suggestion. "Dress up in something cool and royal, something modern."

"But I don't have that kind of clothes," Sasi said, her voice laced with a hint of frustration.

"Hey, use your salary," Rox said, its voice a hint of playful encouragement.

"That's nice," Sasi said, a glimmer of hope returning to her voice.

The taxi pulled up to the club, its bright neon sign a beacon of excitement in the heart of the city.

Dev, his figure sleek and sophisticated in a tailored party coat, stood waiting for Sasi.

"Oh, it's time," Dev said, his eyes scanning the street, his gaze fixed on the arriving taxi.

Sasi, her transformation complete, emerged from the taxi, a vision of elegance and sophistication. She wore a modern, flowing dress, its intricate design a testament to her taste, her beauty enhanced by a subtle, yet striking, makeup.

Dev, caught off guard by her stunning appearance, could only stare.

"You look beautiful, Sasi," Dev said, his voice a mixture of admiration and a touch of awe.

"Shall we go inside, Dev?" Sasi asked, her voice laced with a hint of playful excitement.

"Come on," Dev said, his hand reaching out to take hers.

They stepped inside the club, the music pulsating, the lights flashing, the air thick with anticipation. They walked through a maze of dancing bodies, the beat of the music vibrating through the floor, their steps a rhythmic counterpoint to the throbbing energy of the night.

Sasi's eyes, searching the crowd, spotted Kira. Kira, her movements fluid and graceful, her body a blur of motion, danced in the center of the crowd. The club lights played across her, reflecting off her shimmering dress, and her face, normally stoic, now held a hint of wild abandon as she moved to the music.

Sasi nudged Dev, her eyes sparkling with mischief.

"Hey, Dev," Sasi said, her voice a soft whisper, "Go to her. Dance with her."

"What are you saying?" Dev said, his face a mixture of confusion and a sense of reluctance. "Dance with her? She already hates me."

"But I know you like her," Sasi whispered, her voice laced with a hint of playful conviction.

Sasi, with a gentle push, propelled Dev toward Kira.

Dev, his heart pounding, found himself standing before Kira, the woman who had treated him with such disdain.

"Hey," Dev said, his voice a mixture of nervousness and a hint of a desperate hope. "What, shall we dance together?"

Kira, her gaze fixed on Dev, her expression unreadable, smirked. Her eyes, usually sharp and calculating, now held a flicker of amusement.

"What? Dance together!" she said, her voice dripping with sarcasm. "First, do you know how to dance?"

Kira turned and walked towards the bar, her movements a testament to her indifference, but a small smile played on her lips as she walked away.

Dev, his face filled with a mixture of embarrassment and frustration, turned back to Sasi.

"See, Sasi, she doesn't like me," Dev said, his voice a mixture of sadness and a hint of resignation. "She's got so much ego. What an attitude!"

Sasi, a mischievous glint in her eyes, had an idea.

She grabbed a bottle of alcohol from the bar and handed it to Dev.

"Drink it," Sasi said, her voice a playful command.

Dev, a little hesitant, took the bottle and took a long sip, the taste of alcohol burning his throat, a sudden sense of liberation washing over him.

"What did she say? I know how to dance!" Dev said, his voice a mixture of bravado and a hint of drunken bravado. "Now, I'll show her how to dance."

Dev, a surge of confidence coursing through his veins, stepped onto the dance floor.

His movements, a mix of playful confidence and a hint of uninhibited passion, were a testament to his newfound freedom. He moved with an unexpected grace, his steps fluid and confident, his body responding to the rhythm of the music. The beat of the music seemed to pulse through him, and with each movement, he exuded a newfound confidence, a sense of joyful abandon.

Kira, her eyes fixed on Dev, couldn't help but be captivated by his performance. She watched, her gaze lingering on his every move, a sense of grudging admiration growing within her. She found herself drawn to his energy, to the intensity of his movements, and a flicker of something else, something she hadn't felt in a long time, stirred within her.

Dev's confidence grew, his movements more fluid, his steps more daring. He was a man reborn, his inhibitions shed, his spirit unleashed.

Kira, her own inhibitions melting away, stepped onto the dance floor. The music, now a siren song, pulled her in, and she found herself moving to the beat, her body responding to the energy of the night.

She moved with a grace that mirrored his, her steps a counterpoint to his, their bodies a symphony of movement. The dance floor, a vibrant tapestry of light and movement, swirled around them, the energy of the music a palpable force.

The crowd, caught up in the energy of the dance, surged around them, their bodies moving to the rhythm of the music.

Sasi, her heart pounding, watched as Dev and Kira danced together. She had orchestrated this moment, this meeting, this unexpected connection. The sight of them dancing together, the energy radiating between them, filled her with a sense of relief and a flicker of hope.

She took a sip of alcohol, the taste strong and bitter, the burn a welcome sensation that numbed her senses. The world around her seemed to blur, the music, the lights, the bodies, all blending into a kaleidoscope of movement and sound.

She felt a surge of happiness, a sense of relief. She knew, with a certainty that defied logic, that this moment, this dance, this connection, was a step towards fixing the future.

She joined them, her body moving to the rhythm of the music, her movements a reflection of her own inner turmoil, a mix of joy, anxiety, and a sense of hopeful anticipation.

They danced together, a trio of souls caught in the whirlwind of music and emotion. Their bodies, moving in unison, seemed to defy the chaos that swirled around them. The music, the lights, the dance, they all became a sanctuary, a momentary escape from the realities of their lives.

The music faded, the lights dimmed. The club closed, the energy of the night receding.

Dev, his face a mixture of contentment and a hint of regret, turned to Kira.

"Can I drop you home?" Dev asked, his voice a mixture of hope and uncertainty.

Kira, her face a mixture of amusement and a touch of confusion, shook her head.

"No need," Kira said, her voice a touch slurred. "I can handle myself."

Sasi, her heart filled with a mixture of hope and trepidation, watched them both. Kira, her body swaying slightly, turned to leave, her movements a little unsteady.

Dev, his instincts taking over, reached out to catch her as she stumbled, his fingers brushing against her hand. They made eye contact, their gazes locked for a moment, a mixture of a silent understanding, a hint of a burgeoning attraction, passing between them.

Then, Kira's driver, his presence a reminder of her life outside the club, arrived.

"Let's go, Miss Kira," the driver said, his voice filled with a sense of concern.

Kira, her steps still unsteady, allowed the driver to escort her towards the car.

"Okay, Dev," Sasi said, her voice a mix of sadness and a hint of resignation. "See you later."

Sasi hailed a taxi and climbed in. She watched as Dev, his face filled with a mixture of confusion and a sense of longing, stood by the curb, his gaze fixed on the departing car.

Dev, his heart pounding, his mind racing, pulled out his phone. He received a text message, the address of Sasi's apartment.

He stared at the message, his eyes widening in disbelief. He had a sudden, overwhelming sense of understanding. He had a feeling, a deep sense of certainty, that everything was about to change.

Sasi, her mind a whirlwind of thoughts, looked out the taxi window, her eyes filled with a mixture of confusion and a sense of hope.

She was caught in a game of fate, a game where the rules were constantly shifting, where the consequences of her actions were far-reaching, unpredictable, and devastating.

But she knew, with a certainty that defied logic, that her journey, her adventure, had just begun.

# CHAPTER TWENTY-THREE

# A DANCE OF FATE

next day,The aroma of freshly cooked food filled the small apartment, a welcome comfort in the midst of the chaos that had engulfed Sasi's life. She stirred a pot of fragrant curry, her hands moving with a practiced ease. Beside her, Zara, her pregnant belly a gentle bump beneath her apron, arranged a plate of steaming rice, her movements gentle and deliberate.

"Wow, Sasi, you're a great cook," Zara said, her voice laced with warmth. "The food you made is delicious."

Sasi, her heart warming at Zara's praise, turned to her mother, a genuine smile gracing her lips. "Thanks," Sasi said, her voice laced with a touch of gratitude. "Actually, you're the one who taught me how to cook when I was a child."

Zara, her eyes widening in surprise, looked at Sasi, a mixture of confusion and a sense of wonder crossing her features. "Is that right? Did I really teach you how to cook?" Zara asked, her voice filled with a hint of disbelief.

Sasi laughed, a light, playful sound that echoed through the apartment. She and Zara sat down at the table, their faces filled with a shared joy, their laughter a balm to the pain that had plagued their hearts. They ate in comfortable silence, their eyes meeting every now and then, a shared understanding passing between them.

Suddenly, the doorbell rang, its sound a sharp, unexpected intrusion into the quiet peace of their meal. Sasi, her heart pounding in her chest, her mind racing, rose from the table. Her hand reached for the knob, her eyes fixed on the door.

She opened it, and there he stood. Dev.

Sasi gasped, her eyes widening in disbelief. "Hello, Sasi," Dev said, his smile warm and genuine.

"Dev, you're here?" Sasi said, her voice filled with a mixture of surprise and a sense of unease. "What are you doing here? How did you find my home?"

"Nah, I just asked the taxi driver," Dev said, his smile widening. "Just kidding. The owner... what's her name, huh? Yes, Zara, gave me this address. And she asked me to come here. That's why I'm here."

Sasi, her mind racing, her heart pounding, turned to Zara. "What?" Sasi said, her voice filled with a mixture of disbelief and a sense of unease. "Zara asked you to come here?"

Zara, her smile a mix of mischief and a sense of purpose, walked towards Dev. "Hello, Dev," Zara said, her voice warm and inviting. "You've arrived at the right time. I think this is the perfect time for you two to go to the amusement park tonight."

Sasi's eyes widened in shock. She was confused, her mind struggling to grasp the implications of Zara's words.

"Okay," Dev said, his smile a mix of confusion and amusement. "I'll wait downstairs. Don't wait up for me, Sasi. Hurry."

Dev turned and walked towards the stairs, his footsteps echoing through the apartment.

"But, Mom," Sasi said, her voice laced with a mixture of confusion and a sense of urgency, "Why? Why did you call Dev? And why are you sending us to the amusement park? What's the purpose of this?"

Zara, her smile a mixture of amusement and a sense of purpose, reached out and gently touched Sasi's arm. Zara's eyes, filled with a warmth that Sasi couldn't quite decipher, met Sasi's gaze. "Oh, my dear Sasi," Zara said, her voice filled with a comforting reassurance. "I said that Dev and Kira, your mother-in-law and father-in-law, should fall in love again. You said that's what needed to happen. So, I decided to make a plan."

"Remember, Sasi, where it begins, it should end there," Zara said, her voice filled with a sense of certainty.

Sasi stared at Zara, her mind racing, trying to grasp the implications of her mother's words.

"But what are we going to do at the amusement park?" Sasi asked, her voice a mixture of confusion and a sense of desperation. "How will Dev and Kira meet?"

Zara, her smile widening, chuckled. "My Sasi, I know, I know," Zara said, her eyes twinkling with mischief. "I know that Kira is going to the amusement park tonight. I heard she comes here often."

"What?" Sasi said, her eyes widening in disbelief. "Kira is coming to the amusement park? What?"

From downstairs, Dev's voice called out, "Hey, Sasi, hurry up!"

"Go, Sasi," Zara said, her voice filled with a sense of purpose and a hint of encouragement. "Solve the problem you created. Good luck."

Sasi, her heart pounding in her chest, her mind a whirlwind of thoughts, gave her mother a quick smile and rushed towards the stairs.

She met Dev in the hallway.

"Come on, let's go," Dev said, his smile warm and inviting.

They headed out of the apartment, their footsteps echoing through the hallway, their future uncertain, their hearts filled with a mixture of hope and a sense of foreboding.

They arrived at the amusement park, its brightly lit attractions a kaleidoscope of color, its sounds a symphony of laughter and excitement.

Sasi, her eyes scanning the crowd, her heart pounding in her chest, searched for Kira. She couldn't help but feel a sense of dread. She had unwittingly set in motion a chain of events that had changed the course of history. She had broken the timeline, and now, she had to find a way to fix it.

She needed to get Kira and Dev together, to make sure they fell in love, to ensure that Yash would be born.

But she knew it wouldn't be easy. The amusement park was a labyrinth of twisted paths and unexpected encounters. And the consequences of failure, of altering the future, were too terrible to contemplate.

As the night deepened, the air filled with the scent of cotton candy and the sound of laughter, Sasi, her heart filled with a mixture of hope and fear, stepped into the amusement park, her journey through time far from over.

# CHAPTER TWENTY-FOUR

# THE WHEEL OF DESTINY

The amusement park was a kaleidoscope of flashing lights, boisterous laughter, and the scent of sugar and popcorn. Sasi and Dev, their paths now intertwined by a twist of fate, walked through the throngs of people. Sasi, her gaze constantly scanning the crowd, searched for Kira, her heart pounding with a mixture of hope and trepidation.

Dev, unaware of the weight of Sasi's mission, moved through the park with a gentle kindness. He spotted a group of children huddled together, their faces etched with hunger. Without a word, he approached a nearby food stall, his eyes meeting the vendor's with a silent plea. Moments later, he returned with a tray of steaming hot dogs, his smile warming the faces of the children.

"Here you go, kids," Dev said, his voice laced with a warmth that seemed to melt the anxieties of the children. "Enjoy."

Sasi watched, her heart swelling with a mixture of admiration and a touch of envy. Dev, with his simple act of kindness, had effortlessly touched the lives of those around him, a stark contrast to the cold, ruthless world she had been thrust into.

Sasi noticed a familiar figure, Kira, seated in a solitary cart on the giant Ferris wheel. The Ferris wheel, a majestic structure of steel and lights, reached for the sky, its slow, circular movement a mesmerizing spectacle against the darkening sky.

Sasi, her eyes gleaming with a newfound hope, turned to Dev. She pushed him gently, her voice filled with a sense of urgency.

"Dev, go to the giant wheel ride. Go, Dev."

"Are you not coming?" Dev asked, a hint of confusion lacing his voice.

"I'll come next round," Sasi said, her voice a mixture of a lie and a desperate attempt to ensure that Dev and Kira were alone. "It's too crowded. And I feel dizzy. I'm afraid to ride."

Dev, unaware of the complex web of emotions that drove Sasi's decision, nodded and headed towards the giant wheel. He purchased a ticket, his smile warming the face of the ticket vendor.

But the crowd, eager to ride the giant wheel, surged towards the entrance. Dev, caught in the middle of the jostling throng, found himself pushed towards the last remaining seat, the one beside Kira.

The Ferris wheel operator, his eyes twinkling with a mixture of amusement and a sense of matchmaking, gestured towards the empty seat.

"Sir, please, join the lady for the ride," the operator said, his voice laced with a hint of persuasion.

Dev, his heart pounding in his chest, turned to Kira. She stared back at him, her face a mask of indifference.

They sat side-by-side, the only sound the rhythmic clicking of the giant wheel, their bodies separated by a silent chasm. Their eyes, filled with a mixture of apprehension and a sense of longing, avoiding each other's gaze.

Sasi, watching from below, her heart filled with a mixture of hope and trepidation, couldn't help but feel a surge of optimism.

But the giant wheel, its gears whirring with a mechanical rhythm, suddenly began to shudder. The lights flickered, and the Ferris wheel started to sway, its movement erratic, its ascent interrupted.

Kira, her face a mask of terror, clamored to her ears, her body trembling with fear. She was about to fall unconscious.

Dev, his instincts taking over, reached out to Kira. He wrapped his arms around her, his embrace a protective shield against the chaos. Kira, her body seeking refuge, leaned into his embrace, her head resting against his shoulder.

Her eyes, slowly opening, met Dev's gaze.

Dev, his voice a soothing balm against the backdrop of the whirling Ferris wheel, looked at her, his eyes filled with a mixture of concern and a sense of protectiveness.

"Don't worry," Dev whispered, his voice a low, gentle murmur. "I'm here. I will protect you. Don't be afraid. Hopefully, this ride will be back to normal soon."

Dev held her close, his hands gently caressing her back, his embrace a silent promise of safety.

Moments later, the Ferris wheel lurched to a stop, its ascent halted. The lights flickered back to life, the park's sounds a symphony of chaos and relief.

Dev and Kira, their bodies still intertwined, their gazes locked, exited the Ferris wheel.

Dev, his heart pounding in his chest, his mind reeling from the unexpected intimacy of the moment, looked at Kira.

Kira, her cheeks flushed, her eyes filled with a mixture of confusion and a sense of awakening, returned his gaze.

Sasi, her heart filled with a sense of relief, watched from below, her lips curving into a hopeful smile.

Rox's voice, a mix of excitement and relief, echoed through the park.

"Oh, Sasi, I had a mini-heart attack for a few minutes. Thank God, they're safe. God is great."

"Yeah, Rox," Sasi said, her voice filled with a sense of joy. "God is great. And the words were true. Time and destiny will take care of everything."

But their moment of peace was shattered by a sudden surge of movement. A group of mercenaries, their faces contorted with a chilling intensity, charged towards Kira and Dev, their blades glinting in the moonlight.

"Watch out!" Sasi screamed, her voice filled with a desperate urgency.

Dev, his senses heightened, his body reacting instinctively, turned to face the approaching mercenaries. He moved, his movements a blur of speed and strength, his eyes locked on the men.

He grabbed the mercenary closest to Kira, his grip firm and unwavering, and threw him to the ground. He then turned to face the remaining mercenaries, his eyes burning with a fierce determination.

He caught the second mercenary's arm, twisted it, and then punched him, sending the man crashing into the crowd. He then grabbed the third mercenary, twisting his neck, and kicked him away, his movements a display of raw power.

The crowd, filled with a mixture of terror and a sense of disbelief, scattered, their cries echoing through the park.

Aryan, his face a mask of rage, his eyes burning with a cold, unyielding fury, emerged from the crowd, his blade glinting in the moonlight, his footsteps heavy and deliberate. He headed towards Kira, Dev, and Sasi.

# CHAPTER TWENTY-FIVE

# THE PRICE OF TIME

The amusement park, once a haven of laughter and light, now echoed with the chilling silence of a battlefield. Aryan, his face a mask of rage, moved towards Kira and Dev, his blade glinting in the moonlight, his steps heavy and deliberate.

The mercenaries, their faces contorted with a chilling intensity, charged forward, their blades glinting in the moonlight, their movements a blur of violence.

Dev, his body reacting instinctively, turned to face the approaching mercenaries. He moved, his movements a blur of speed and strength, his eyes locked on the men.

He caught the first mercenary's arm, twisted it, and then punched him, sending the man crashing into the crowd. He then grabbed the second mercenary, twisting his neck, and kicked him away, his movements a display of raw power.

Sasi, her heart pounding in her chest, watched with a mixture of terror and a sense of admiration. She knew Dev was no trained fighter, but in this moment, he was a whirlwind of power, a force of nature unleashed.

He faced the mercenary leader, a hulking brute with a face that seemed to have been carved out of granite. The mercenary leader, his eyes filled with a chilling intensity, charged towards Dev, his arms swinging, his movements a blur of violence.

Dev, his body a blur of motion, dodged the mercenary's attack, his movements precise and calculated. He waited for the perfect moment, his eyes locked on the mercenary's every move.

Then, with a swift, powerful move, Dev grabbed the mercenary's arm, his grip firm and unyielding. He twisted the arm, breaking the bone with a sickening crunch.

Then, with a devastating kick, he sent the mercenary crashing to the ground. The mercenary leader screamed in agony, his body writhing in pain.

The remaining mercenaries, their leader defeated, their confidence shattered, turned and fled. They ran towards the exit, their movements a chaotic scramble, their eyes filled with fear.

They removed the blockade they had created, the gate swinging open, the parking area accessible once again. They carried their leader away, their faces a mixture of defeat and a sense of urgent escape.

Sasi, her breath catching in her throat, watched as the mercenaries disappeared, their retreat a testament to Dev's unexpected power.

She turned to Dev, a sense of gratitude and awe filling her heart. She had witnessed his courage, his strength, his resilience.

She had a feeling, a sense of certainty, that this encounter, this moment of unexpected heroism, was going to change everything.

But before Sasi could fully embrace the sense of relief that washed over her, Aryan, his face contorted with rage, kicked Dev from behind.

Dev stumbled forward, his body crashing to the ground. He turned, his eyes meeting Aryan's, a mixture of anger and a sense of disbelief filling his features.

Dev, his fists clenched, charged towards Aryan, his movements fueled by a surge of adrenaline. But Aryan, his movements a blur of speed, easily deflected Dev's attacks.

Aryan, a man who had built his empire on violence, was a master of physical combat. He was a whirlwind of power, a force of nature unleashed.

"Have you done enough?" Aryan said, his voice laced with a mixture of arrogance and a chilling amusement. "So, you're the guy who beat my men at the office, huh? I believe they were beaten by a joker like you."

Dev, his anger rising, dashed forward, his fists aimed at Aryan's face. But Aryan, his movements swift and decisive, caught Dev's fist, twisted it, and then sent Dev crashing to the ground with a powerful kick.

As the two men grappled, the Nexus watch, the very device that had shattered the timeline, slipped from Aryan's wrist. The watch crashed to the ground, its sleek silver surface shattering, its intricate mechanisms exposed.

Sasi, her eyes fixed on the watch, didn't notice the watch had broken. Her attention was focused solely on the scene unfolding before her.

Aryan, his anger reaching a fever pitch, beat Dev mercilessly. Dev, his body wracked with pain, was unable to defend himself.

Aryan, his eyes burning with a cold fury, raised his blade, its sharp edge glinting in the moonlight. He brought the blade down, slashing Dev across the back, the sound of the blade slicing through flesh a sickening, chilling sound.

"Nooo," Kira screamed, her voice filled with a mixture of horror and a sense of desperation.

Sasi, her heart pounding in her chest, rushed towards Dev and Aryan.

Aryan, his movements swift and brutal, raised the blade again, his eyes locked on Dev.

But just as he was about to strike, Kira stepped between them.

Aryan, his movements a blur of speed, brought the blade down, his blade catching Kira's head.

Kira and Dev, their bodies crumpling to the ground, fell unconscious.

The sirens wailed in the distance, the sound a beacon of hope amidst the chaos.

Aryan, his eyes scanning the crowd, noticed the police approaching. He turned and ran, his men close behind him.

As Aryan disappeared into the darkness, he looked back at Sasi, his eyes filled with a chilling intensity.

"Remember, this is not the end, girl," Aryan said, his voice a low, threatening growl. "I will come for you! And you will pay for what you've done! And I will show you who you've messed with!"

The mercenaries, their faces a mixture of fear and a sense of urgency, hurried to their leader's side, their movements a desperate attempt to escape the approaching police.

Sasi, her heart filled with a mixture of fear and a sense of overwhelming despair, knelt beside Dev and Kira. She reached out, her hands gently caressing their faces.

She couldn't believe what she had seen. She had failed to protect them.

She saw the Nexus watch, shattered and broken, lying on the ground. She picked it up, her fingers trembling.

"Oh, no, no," Sasi whispered, her voice filled with a sense of panic. "This can't be happening. Please, turn on."

She desperately tried to activate the watch, but it was beyond repair.

Rox, its voice filled with a sense of urgency, said, "Sasi, Sasi, emergency. My power is going off. I don't know why. It seems like I've used up all the power I got from the future. Please, Sasi. Do something. I don't want to leave you."

"Oh, no, no," Sasi cried, her voice filled with a sense of despair. "Rox, you can't leave me. Please stay with me."

Sasi, her heart pounding in her chest, collapsed to the ground, her body racked with sobs.

The police arrived, their blue lights flashing, their sirens wailing. They quickly apprehended the unconscious Dev and Kira, carrying them towards an ambulance.

Sasi, her mind reeling, her body heavy with a sense of despair, followed them, her steps slow and hesitant.

The police officers, their faces etched with a mixture of concern and suspicion, asked Sasi what had happened, but she remained silent, her body a statue of grief, her mind consumed by a sense of overwhelming guilt.

The ambulance sped towards the hospital, its siren a mournful wail.

Sasi, her eyes filled with tears, watched as the ambulance disappeared into the night.

At the hospital, the doctor, his face grim, told the police officers that Dev and Kira's conditions were critical.

"We need more time to say what will happen," the doctor said, his voice laced with a sense of uncertainty.

Sasi, her eyes filled with a mixture of guilt and a deep sense of sadness, looked at Dev and Kira, their bodies lying still on the hospital beds, their faces pale and lifeless.

She left the hospital, her steps heavy, her heart filled with a crushing sense of despair.

The sky outside was a canvas of darkness, the wind howling, the rain pouring down in sheets.

Sasi, her body trembling, reached her apartment, its interior dimly lit, its silence a stark contrast to the storm raging outside.

She knelt on the floor, her body wracked with sobs.

"What have I done?" Sasi whispered, her voice barely audible over the sound of her own tears. "I don't know what to do now? I lost the chance. I missed every chance I got. And I failed them. I failed them all."

Sasi reached into her pocket, her fingers brushing against the broken Nexus watch. She pulled it out, its shattered surface reflecting the dim light of the apartment.

"It's all because of this stupid watch," Sasi said, her voice filled with a mixture of anger and a sense of despair.

She threw the watch across the room, its broken pieces clattering against the wall, a symbol of her failure, her despair, her shattered dreams.

"I lost everything," Sasi whispered, her voice choked with sobs. "I have no reason to live. Sorry, Mom. Sorry, Yash. Sorry to my parents-in-law. I failed to save them, to keep your faith."

Sasi, her body wracked with sobs, looked around the room. Her eyes fell on a knife, its blade gleaming under the dim light of the apartment. She picked it up, its metal surface cold and unforgiving in her hand.

Then, a montage of images flashed before her eyes.

A dark, stormy night.

A deserted amusement park, its lights flickering in the darkness.

The faces of Dev and Kira, their bodies lying still, their faces pale and lifeless.

The brutal image of Aryan, his face contorted with a chilling rage, his blade dripping with blood.

Sasi, her legs wounded, her body trembling, her eyes filled with a mixture of despair and a sense of resignation, walked towards the mirror. She held the knife, its cold metal pressing against her skin.

She closed her eyes, her face filled with a mixture of guilt and a sense of hopeless despair.

"Why?" Sasi whispered, her voice barely audible over the roar of the storm. "Why did it all come to this? It's all my fault. I'm responsible. I had no choice. I lost everything. I have nothing left."

The image of the mercenaries, their faces masks of darkness, their bodies a menacing silhouette, emerged from the shadows. They moved towards her, their steps heavy, their presence a palpable threat.

The montage faded, the image of the broken watch, its shattered surface a symbol of her shattered dreams, remaining imprinted on her mind.

Sasi, her body trembling, her eyes filled with a mix of despair and a sense of resignation, raised the knife to her throat.

Her life, her future, her dreams, had been irrevocably shattered by the Nexus watch, a device designed to unlock the secrets of time, a device that had instead become a weapon of destruction, a tool that had irrevocably altered the course of history.

# THE PRICE OF A STOLEN MOMENT

The mirror reflected Sasi's image, a haunting silhouette bathed in the dim light of the apartment. Her eyes were red-rimmed, her face etched with a mixture of despair and regret. The knife, a cold, unyielding metal, rested against her throat, a silent testament to the pain that consumed her.

Suddenly, her grip loosened, the knife clattering to the floor with a metallic clang. She closed her eyes, tears streaming down her face, her sobs muffled by her trembling hands.

"Yash," she whispered, her voice barely audible, choked by the torrent of emotions that surged through her. "I'm sorry... I... love... you."

The scene shifted, reeling back to a time of youthful innocence, a time of stolen glances and whispered dreams.

Sasi, a young woman with a vibrant energy, practiced her athletic drills on the college field. She wore a tight sports uniform, her movements fluid and graceful, her face flushed with exertion.

Across the field, a group of young men, their faces alight with a mixture of admiration and a hint of disrespect, watched the girls. They made crude jokes, their words laced with a sense of entitlement.

Sasi, her ears catching the whispers of their words, turned around, her eyes narrowed, her face a mixture of anger and disgust.

She decided to confront them, to stand up for herself and for the other girls.

She started to walk towards the boys, her steps determined, her heart pounding with a mixture of indignation and a sense of righteous fury.

But before she could reach them, a wave of movement.

A figure, his steps sure and swift, moved towards the group of boys, his face a mask of simmering rage.

The boys, caught off guard by the sudden intrusion, turned around, their faces contorting with fear. They saw him, Yash, a young man with a piercing gaze and an undeniable aura of authority.

Yash, without a word, delivered a powerful kick to the lead boy's back, the impact sending the boy crashing to the ground. He then turned to the remaining boys, his voice filled with a simmering rage.

"You bastards!" Yash roared, his voice a thunderclap of fury. "What are you talking about? Respect them. This is your last warning. Now, go to class!"

The boys, terrified, scrambled to their feet, their faces etched with a mixture of fear and shame. They ran away, their retreat a chaotic scramble.

Yash, his anger still simmering, turned to leave.

Sasi, her heart pounding in her chest, her eyes fixed on Yash, found herself mesmerized. She had witnessed his strength, his courage, his unwavering conviction.

She tried to follow him, her footsteps carrying her towards the bustling crowd, but she lost sight of him.

The next day, Sasi sat in the college assembly, her eyes scanning the crowd, her heart pounding with a mixture of anticipation and a hint of disappointment. She was searching for him, for Yash.

The principal of the college, his voice booming through the auditorium, announced the topper of the college, the student of the year.

The crowd erupted in applause.

"And here he comes," the principal said, his voice filled with pride. "Mr. Yash."

Yash, his face beaming with a mixture of pride and humility, walked towards the stage.

Sasi, her eyes wide with a mixture of shock and admiration, recognized him.

"It's him," Sasi thought, her heart pounding in her chest. "Oh, his name is Yash."

She stared at him, her gaze lingering on his face, her heart pounding with a newfound admiration.

Sasi, caught in the whirlwind of her emotions, fell in love.

Days turned into weeks, weeks into months. Sasi watched Yash from a distance, her heart filled with a sense of shy adoration. She always found herself blushing whenever their eyes met.

She was completely and utterly in love with him.

A few years later after college life , Zara and Kira, her mother and mother-in-law, arranged a marriage for Sasi and Yash.

After Kira and Dev had left, Zara turned to Sasi.

"Sasi, I have seen your groom. See his photo," Zara said, her eyes filled with a mixture of hope and a sense of excitement.

"What?" Sasi asked, her voice laced with a mixture of surprise and apprehension. "Married? For me? Why did you do this, Mom? I'm not interested in marriage."

Zara, her smile unwavering, handed Sasi a photograph.

"Sasi, the guy's name is Yash, and he...," Zara began, but Sasi's eyes widened in disbelief.

Sasi snatched the photograph from her mother's hand, her fingers trembling with a mixture of excitement and a sense of surreal disbelief.

She opened the photograph, her eyes fixed on the man in the picture. It was Yash, her crush, her secret love.

Sasi's face, transformed by a surge of joy, beamed with happiness. She threw her arms around her mother, her embrace filled with a sense of overwhelming joy.

She ran towards her room, her steps light, her heart overflowing with a mixture of anticipation and a sense of unreal joy.

She slammed the door shut behind her, her movements a blur of excitement.

She threw herself onto the bed, her body a whirlwind of happiness. She stared at the photograph of Yash, her eyes filled with a sense of awe, her heart overflowing with love.

"Finally, you're going to be mine, my sweetheart," Sasi whispered, her voice filled with a mixture of joy and a sense of accomplishment. "Thank you, God. I'll never lose him. I'll always stay with him. I'll take care of him, no matter what."

She leaned towards the photograph, her lips brushing against Yash's image, her eyes filled with a deep, unwavering love.

"I love you," she whispered, her voice filled with a sense of absolute certainty.

The flashback faded, the scene shifting back to the present.

Sasi, her heart pounding, her mind reeling, stood at the edge of her own existence. She had stumbled through a maze of time, a labyrinth of twists and turns, a journey that had unveiled a past she had never known.

She knew that this was just the beginning. The future was uncertain, the path ahead shrouded in mystery.

But she knew that she had found a strength she never knew she possessed. She had faced her fears, confronted her past, and discovered a love that transcended the boundaries of time.

Outside, a car pulled up, its engine a low, throbbing hum. Aryan, his face a mask of cold determination, stepped out of the car. He started to walk towards the apartment building, his steps deliberate, his eyes fixed on the destination.

Zara, her heart pounding, her instincts warning her of the danger, saw Aryan from her window. She watched as he was joined by a group of mercenaries, their forms a menacing tableau of shadows and steel.

She knew that Aryan was coming for Sasi. She had to protect her, to shield her daughter from the storm that was brewing.

Zara, her movements quick and determined, hurried towards Sasi's room, her heart filled with a mixture of fear and a mother's fierce protectiveness.

She knew that the battle for her daughter's future had just begun.

# CHAPTER TWENTY-SEVEN

# THE SHADOW OF HOPE

The mirror reflected Sasi's image, a haunting silhouette bathed in the dim light of the apartment. Her eyes, red-rimmed and filled with despair, stared back at her. The knife, a cold, unyielding metal, pressed against her throat, the weight of her despair a physical force.

She closed her eyes, a silent plea escaping her lips. "Yash... I'm so sorry... I... love... you." The words, choked by sobs, were a final act of reconciliation, a desperate attempt to find peace before the darkness consumed her.

But then, a sudden change.

The knife slipped from her grasp, clattering to the floor, the metallic sound a jarring echo in the silent room.

Sasi, her body wracked with a wave of emotion, dropped to her knees. Her sobs, muffled by her trembling hands, echoed through the oppressive silence.

"No, no, I can't kill myself," she cried, her voice raw with despair, her words a desperate plea for redemption. "I'm sorry, everyone. Please forgive me."

Outside the door, a rhythmic pounding, a relentless hammering, shattered the silence. The sound was a harbinger of doom, a chilling reminder of the danger that lurked beyond the threshold.

Sasi's breath hitched in her throat. Her fingers dug into the worn fabric of the sofa as she stared at the splintering wood of the door, her eyes widening with each crack. A wave of cold dread washed over her. The scent of dust and fear filled the air, a chilling premonition of the violence that awaited her.

The door splintered, a harsh, splintering sound that pierced the silence. Two figures, their faces hidden in the shadows, surged into the room. Their blades, glinting menacingly under the faint glow of the streetlights filtering through the window, seemed to cut through the darkness.

Sasi, her body frozen with fear, watched as the mercenaries approached. She couldn't fight, couldn't run. She could only accept the inevitable.

But then, a sudden shift in the energy.

The air crackled with a surge of power, a sudden shift in the atmosphere, a palpable sense of impending change.

Sasi, her body heavy with exhaustion, her mind filled with a sense of surrender, collapsed onto the floor, her consciousness fading.

The mercenaries, their blades poised to strike, moved forward. They were about to end Sasi's life, but in that moment, a shadow, a figure shrouded in darkness, appeared.

He moved with a speed that defied comprehension, his form a blur of motion. The air around him crackled with energy, a symphony of power and darkness. He caught Sasi in his arms, lifting her, shielding her from the mercenaries' blades.

He stopped the mercenaries' advance, his hands gripping their arms, his movements a symphony of power.

He twisted the mercenaries' arms, the bones snapping with a sickening crunch. He then delivered a powerful kick to their chests, sending them flying backward, their bodies crashing into the wall, the sound echoing through the room.

The remaining mercenaries, their eyes wide with disbelief and fear, stumbled backward, their movements a chaotic scramble.

The figure, his form a mixture of light and shadow, gently placed Sasi on the floor, his movements filled with a sense of care and concern. He then moved towards the mercenaries, his eyes burning with a cold, intense fury.

He stood before them, his form a chilling tableau of power, a mixture of darkness and light. Lightning, flashing outside, illuminated the room, casting his figure in an eerie, ethereal glow. The air crackled, the scent of ozone filling the room, a palpable sense of power emanating from the figure.

Sasi, her consciousness flickering back, saw a blur, a fleeting image, a glimpse of the figure who had saved her. His black and violet over coat, a striking contrast against the darkness, was a testament to his power. The faint glow of the lightning illuminated the coat, casting a ghostly, otherworldly sheen upon it.

She was too weak, too exhausted, to see his face. But she knew, with a certainty that defied logic, that it was Yash.

She gasped, her breath catching in her throat. She closed her eyes, a wave of relief washing over her, and then, she succumbed to the darkness.

Yash, his face a mask of anger and determination, stood before the mercenaries, his eyes blazing with a cold, intense fury.

He raised his hand, his palm open, his fingers spread. He beckoned them closer, his eyes a chilling mix of power and a sense of terrifying inevitability.

"Come," Yash said, his voice a low, threatening growl. The air crackled with anticipation, the silence punctuated by the rhythmic beat of his heart.

# CHAPTER TWENTY-EIGHT

# THE WEIGHT OF TRUTH

The flashback unfolds in 2050, The city lights, a dazzling kaleidoscope of neon and glass, painted the night sky in vibrant hues, but the darkness held a chilling silence. Yash, his mind a whirlwind of emotions, replayed the events of the past few days, the truth of Sasi's actions unfolding before him like a tragic, unfolding drama.

He had been at the lab, his focus entirely on the Nexus watch, his mind consumed by the relentless pursuit of his ambition, when a chill had run down his spine, a sudden, unexplainable feeling of dread. He had tried to ignore it, to push it aside, but the fear had persisted, a persistent whisper in the back of his mind.

He had picked up his phone, a desperate attempt to connect with Sasi, to hear her voice, to feel her presence, but there was no answer.

Then, the phone call.

The doctor's words, a chilling echo of reality.

"Hello, Mr. Yash," the doctor had said, his voice warm and professional, "How are you?"

"What's up, doctor?" Yash had responded, a forced cheerfulness in his voice, a mask for the anxiety that gnawed at him.

"I'm great, Yash. I called you to say something important," the doctor had said, his voice taking on a serious tone.

"What's the matter, doctor?" Yash had asked, a knot of apprehension tightening in his stomach.

"Yash, Mr. Yash," the doctor had said, his voice filled with a mixture of congratulations and concern. "You're going to be a father. And your wife, Sasi, is going to be a mother. You're going to be parents."

Yash was stunned. His mind struggled to process the information, his emotions a jumble of disbelief and an overwhelming sense of joy.

"Yes, Yash," the doctor had said, his voice filled with a gentle reassurance. "Your wife is pregnant. She's been visiting the hospital for checkups. We discovered she's expecting. Take care of your wife, Sasi, Mr. Yash."

"Okay, doctor, thank you for the information. I'll take care of my wife," Yash had said, a surge of happiness washing over him, a genuine smile spreading across his face.

He had ended the call, his heart overflowing with joy, his mind filled with images of a future he had never imagined. He couldn't hold back the happiness that bubbled within him.

But then, another call.

A different voice, a voice that resonated with authority, a voice that held the promise of both help and a chilling revelation.

"Hello, Mr. Yash," Mr. V had said, his voice laced with a gentle warmth. "Nice to meet you, my boy. A brilliant mind."

"Hello, sir," Yash had responded, his voice filled with gratitude. "It's nice to meet you too, sir. Sir, thank you so much for believing in me and my project. Thank you for supporting me. I'm so grateful to you. I wish I could thank you in person, sir."

Mr. V had laughed softly, a gentle, knowing sound. "Yeah, yeah, Yash. I'm proud to help you. But I have to tell you something, Yash."

"Yes, sir," Yash had said, his voice filled with anticipation. "You can tell me."

"Mr. Yash," Mr. V had said, his voice dropping to a more serious tone. "It's actually not me who deserves this encouragement and thanks. It actually belongs to someone special to you."

Yash was shocked. "What, sir? What are you talking about? Who is this person?"

"It's actually your wife, Sasi, Mr. Yash."

Yash's mind raced, trying to understand, to make sense of the doctor's words. He had believed that the success of his project was a testament to his own hard work, his own ingenuity. But now, he was being told that Sasi, his wife, the woman he had taken for granted, the woman he had neglected, was the one who had made it all possible.

Mr. V then recounted the story of Sasi's visit to his office, her determination, her eloquence, her unwavering belief in Yash and his project.

**The scene shifted to Mr. V's office. Sasi, her face determined, her voice filled with a desperate urgency, stood before Mr. V's assistant. **

"Please, sir," Sasi had pleaded, her voice laced with desperation. "Let me see Mr. V. Please, sir."

The assistant, his eyes filled with a sense of indifference, shook his head. "No, it's not possible right now. Please leave. You can't see him without an appointment."

Sasi's voice, its tone shifting from a plea to a demand, grew in strength. "Hey, get out of the way," Sasi said, her voice laced with a hint of authority, a newfound confidence. "This is very important. Just let me in. Can't you understand?"

Mr. V, his eyes fixed on his computer screen, heard the commotion outside his office. He paused, his brow furrowed, and called out to his assistant.

"What's the matter?" Mr. V asked, his voice laced with a hint of irritation. "Who's that woman? And why are you arguing with her?"

"Nothing, sir," the assistant responded, his voice a little hesitant. "She said she wanted to meet you."

"Okay," Mr. V said, his voice softened by a hint of curiosity. "Tell her to come in."

Sasi, her heart pounding, entered the office. She walked towards Mr. V's desk, her gaze fixed on the man behind it.

Mr. V(41), his face a mix of kindness and a sense of curiosity, turned towards Sasi. He was a man of about forty-one, his face etched with the lines of time and experience.

"Hello, Madam," Mr. V said, his voice filled with a gentle warmth. "How can I help you? What's the reason you wanted to see me?"

Sasi, her eyes fixed on Mr. V's face, felt a strange sensation.

"Sir, you... I think I've seen you before," Sasi said, her voice a mixture of surprise and a sense of bewilderment.

"Me? Where?" Mr. V asked, his eyes filled with a mixture of amusement and a hint of confusion.

"Yes, I got it," Sasi said, her voice a little shaky. "Do you remember me? Years ago, when I was a little girl. I think you must have been about twenty-one. You were on a bus, and you helped me blow up a balloon. You remember me, sir. I was that little girl."

"Oh, my..." Mr. V said, his eyes widening in recognition. "I remember that day. I'll never forget it. It was the first day of my college. And that cute little girl, that was you. And I remember, after I met you, my life completely changed. It went on a beautiful path. Please, sit down. What's your name?"

Sasi, her heart filled with a mixture of joy and a sense of wonder, sat down on the chair.

"My name is Sasi," she said, her voice filled with a sense of gratitude. "It's nice to see you, sir."

"It's nice to meet you too," Mr. V said, his smile genuine.

Sasi then told Mr. V everything. She explained Yash's struggles, his relentless pursuit of his dream project, his frustration with the rejection he had faced. She spoke of Yash's passion, his dedication, his brilliant mind. She described Yash's love for her, his unwavering commitment to his dreams, and his heartbreaking isolation.

Mr. V listened intently, his eyes filled with a mix of sympathy and understanding. He had seen this type of struggle before. He had been in a similar situation, a young man with a dream, a dream that had taken him on a journey far beyond the ordinary.

When Sasi finished, Mr. V said, "Don't worry, Sasi. I'll help your husband. It's my responsibility to help you. Because you helped me when you were a little girl, and now it's my turn to help you. Don't worry, I'll take care of this."

"Thank you, sir," Sasi said, her voice filled with a sense of gratitude. "Sir, you must come to our house one day. Let's celebrate, have dinner together, with your family, okay?"

Mr. V, his face beaming with a genuine warmth, stood up.

"Oh, sure, Sasi," Mr. V said, his voice filled with a sense of enthusiasm. "I will come to your house with my family."

They shook hands, a bond of gratitude and connection forged between them.

Mr. V then ended the call.

Yash, his mind reeling, his heart filled with a mixture of disbelief and a sense of overwhelming gratitude, was left speechless.

"So, Mr. Yash," Mr. V had said, his voice filled with a mix of warmth and a sense of gentle guidance. "First, thank your wife. Because if she hadn't come to me, I wouldn't have helped you. Your project wouldn't have been approved. So thank her. Also, Yash, she loves you very much. She's ready to do anything for you. Don't ever miss out on a woman like her. And now, let's hang up."

Yash, his mind still spinning, his heart filled with a mixture of regret and a desperate hope, hung up the phone.

"How can I tell Mom and Dad?" Yash thought, his voice a silent whisper, his heart heavy with the weight of his guilt.

Kira and Dev entered the room, their faces filled with concern.

"Yash, where is Sasi?" Kira asked, her voice laced with a hint of impatience.

"Huh, actually, Mom," Yash said, his voice a mixture of forced cheerfulness and a desperate attempt to hide his true emotions. "She said she wanted to see her Mom. So, I dropped her off at her Mom's house. She'll be back soon. But it's taking a bit long."

"Okay, okay, Yash," Kira said, her voice filled with a mixture of reassurance and a touch of worry. "Let Sasi stay at her Mom's. But remember, Yash, don't forget to bring her back. Tell her to come fast. We miss her."

"Okay, Mom, Dad," Yash said, his voice a low murmur, his eyes fixed on the floor.

Yash went to his room, his movements heavy, his mind consumed by the weight of his actions. He closed the door behind him, locking it. He threw himself onto the bed, his anger and frustration bubbling to the surface.

He began to push and break the furniture, his movements a violent outburst of emotion.

"What do I do now?" he screamed, his voice filled with a sense of desperate urgency. "How can I save her?"

He knealed on the floor, his body wracked with sobs.

Then, a cardboard box fell from a broken shelf, landing at Yash's feet. He picked up the box, his fingers tracing the worn surface. He opened the box, his eyes widening in disbelief. Inside, he found a collection of photographs, love letters, and tokens of affection.

These were the things that Sasi had kept, the memories of their time together, a tangible reminder of her love for him.

He picked up a photograph, his eyes meeting Sasi's in the picture. She was beautiful, her eyes sparkling with a mixture of joy and mischief. He could almost hear her laughter, feel the warmth of her presence.

He took the picture and held it close to his heart, tears streaming down his face.

"I'm sorry, Sasi," Yash said, his voice choked with emotion. "I didn't understand your love and care. I'll find a way to bring you back. I promise, I'll take care of you, I'll be the person you want me to be. I promise."

# CHAPTER TWENTY-NINE

# THE ECHO OF A PROMISE

The days turned into weeks, the weeks into months. Yash, driven by a relentless sense of purpose, focused on rebuilding the Nexus watch. He worked tirelessly, his mind consumed by the need to fix the future, to undo the mistakes he had made.

But he couldn't forget Sasi.

He often visited the beach, their favorite spot, the place where they had shared their first kiss. He sat there, watching the waves crash against the shore, his eyes searching the horizon, his heart filled with a longing for her touch, her laughter, her presence.

The salty air, the sound of the waves, the vastness of the ocean, they all brought back memories, fragments of a shared past, a life that now seemed so distant, so impossible.

He had lost her, his Sasi, his love.

But he wouldn't give up.

Finally, Yash completed the Nexus watch. He stood before it, his eyes filled with a mixture of determination and a sense of hopeful anticipation.

He picked up the watch, its silver surface gleaming under the lab lights. He then pulled on the black and violet coat that Sasi had chosen for him, the coat that had been a symbol of their connection, a reminder of her love.

"Finally, the watch is ready," Yash said, his voice filled with a sense of purpose. "And I've found her location and the time she went to. Rox, the bracelet she's wearing helped me track her. The watch and the bracelet are interconnected. I'm coming for you, Sasi. Don't worry."

He slipped the watch onto his wrist, its metal band cool against his skin. He then stepped into the time vortex, its swirling energy a gateway to a world beyond his comprehension.

He closed his eyes, his mind focused on his destination, his heart filled with a mixture of love and a sense of unwavering determination.

He landed in the restroom of the club.

Yash stepped out of the restroom, his eyes scanning the room. The club was a symphony of sound and light, a vibrant tapestry of dancing bodies and flashing lights. He had expected to land in the place where Sasi was, but this was not the place he anticipated.

"What is this place?" Yash asked, his voice filled with a sense of confusion. "Why did I come here? I should have landed where Sasi was."

He stepped out of the restroom, his heart pounding. He looked around, his eyes widening in disbelief.

"What?" Yash whispered, his voice filled with a mixture of shock and a sense of bewilderment. "A night dance club party place?"

He scanned the dance floor, his eyes searching for any sign of Sasi. Then, he saw them.

His father, Dev, a younger version of himself, was standing by the bar. Dev, his face a mirror image of his own, exuded a confident charm, his movements fluid and graceful.

Yash, his mind racing, could only stare.

"What?" Yash whispered, his voice filled with a mixture of shock and disbelief. "That guy? We have the same face?"

He reached out, his hand instinctively touching his own face, his eyes searching for any difference, any anomaly.

Then, he saw her. Kira, a younger version of his mother, her face a striking mirror image of his own, stood across the room, her gaze fixed on Dev.

Yash was stunned.

"They both look like my Mom and Dad," Yash thought, his mind reeling, his heart pounding with a sense of disbelief. "Dev and Kira? What's happening here?"

He looked at a calendar on the wall.

"Oh, dear," Yash thought, his mind filled with a sense of overwhelming certainty. "I've come back twenty-five years in the past."

He knew he had to find Sasi.

He watched as Sasi, a radiant smile on her face, talked to his father, Dev. They seemed to know each other well, their conversation filled with a casual familiarity.

Then, he watched as they danced. The three of them, Sasi, Dev, and Kira, moved together, their bodies a symphony of movement, their laughter echoing through the club.

Yash, his heart filled with a mix of joy and a sense of overwhelming sadness, watched. He couldn't believe what he was seeing.

He waited, his eyes fixed on Sasi, until the party ended. Then, he tried to catch up with her. But Sasi, her movements swift and graceful, hailed a taxi and left.

Yash, his mind racing, spotted an abandoned motorcycle. He jumped on the bike, his heart pounding, his mind focused on Sasi.

He followed the taxi, his eyes fixed on its rear lights, his heart filled with a sense of urgent determination.

He followed the taxi to her apartment. He tried to approach Sasi, but she hurried into her room and locked the door.

He reached out, his hand reaching for the door, but before he could touch it, a woman's hand grabbed him from behind.

"Hey, stop!" the woman said, her voice laced with a mixture of surprise and a hint of annoyance. "Where are you going? Who are you?"

She took a closer look at Yash, her eyes widening in disbelief.

"Oh, Dev, it's you," the woman said, her voice a mix of surprise and a sense of relief. "What's up? How are you? You came to see Sasi?"

"Wait, you," Yash said, his voice a mixture of shock and a sense of dawning understanding.

"I'm the owner of this apartment," the woman said, her smile a mixture of warmth and a sense of amusement. "And I'm a good friend of Sasi."

Yash's mind raced, trying to piece together the puzzle. "Wait, you must be Sasi's mother. She's young too, like my Mom and Dad. And you thought I was my father, I think," Yash thought, his heart filled with a sense of confusion and a growing sense of urgency.

"Hey," Yash said, his voice a mixture of nervousness and a sense of desperate hope. "Nice to meet you. I'd like to ask you a few questions."

"Oh, yes, come into my room, Dev," the woman said, her gaze fixed on Yash, her smile a welcoming gesture.

Yash and the woman entered her room.

"So, Dev, what's your question?" the woman asked, her eyes filled with curiosity, her voice laced with a hint of playful warmth.

Yash, his face a mixture of guilt and a sense of desperate honesty, looked at the woman.

"Actually, I'm not Dev," Yash said, his voice a mixture of nervousness and a sense of desperate hope.

The woman, her eyes widening in disbelief, could only stare at him.

"What?" she said, her voice filled with a mix of shock and confusion. "You're Dev? Who are you? Are you joking?"

"I know you can't believe what I'm saying, but I'm telling you the truth. I'm not Dev," Yash said, his voice filled with a sense of urgency. "I'm Yash, the son of Dev and Kira, the inventor of the time watch, and the husband of my loveable wife, Sasi Rekha."

The woman was stunned.

"What?" the woman said, her voice filled with a mix of disbelief and a sense of recognition. "You're the Yash that Sasi told me about?"

"What did Sasi tell you?" Yash asked, his voice laced with a mixture of desperation and a hint of pleading. "I don't understand. Please, tell me everything that happened here. Why is Sasi helping my father, Dev, and my mother, Kira, now, in the past?"

Zara, the woman who was standing before him, had lived a life filled with secrets and a burden of sacrifice. She shared the story of her life, her love for Aryan, his descent into darkness, and the choices she had made to protect herself and her child. She told Yash about Sasi's arrival in the past, her accidental interference with the timeline, and her unwavering dedication to saving those she loved.

Yash, his heart heavy, his mind racing, listened intently, his eyes filled with a mixture of awe, regret, and a sense of overwhelming love.

After Zara finished her story, Yash was silent, his eyes filled with tears.

"Yeah," Zara said, her voice laced with a mix of sadness and a sense of resigned acceptance. "She's literally carrying the entire timeline now, like a nexus being between timelines and her own personal reality. And she's doing all of this for your mother and father, to be together. And more than that, she's doing all of this for the person she loves the most in this world. That person is you, Yash. She's taken all these risks for you."

"Yeah," Yash said, his voice choked with emotion. "I feel proud and guilty. I'm one of the reasons why Sasi is facing all these problems. I have to solve this, I have to help her."

Yash, his heart filled with a renewed sense of purpose, turned to leave.

Zara stopped him.

"Wait, Yash, don't go to Sasi's room," Zara said, her voice laced with a sense of urgency. "It's not the right time to see her."

"Why?" Yash asked, his brow furrowed with concern.

"There's a threat, Yash," Zara said, her voice filled with a sense of foreboding. "Aryan is trying to kill both your parents and your wife. Wait."

"Aryan?" Yash asked, his face hardening with a mixture of anger and a sense of protective determination.

"Yes," Zara whispered, her head bowed, her voice laced with a mixture of fear and a sense of helpless resignation. "He'll try to kill them."

"I will save them. I will protect them from Aryan. I'll protect them, even if it means becoming a shadow, a ghost in the night," Yash said, his voice filled with a sense of unwavering conviction. "And, Mrs. Zara, please forgive me if I kill your husband, my wife's father. Don't worry."

"It's okay, Yash," Zara said, her eyes filled with a sense of desperate hope. "Kill that monster."

Yash, his face a mask of determination, nodded.

"We'll see who kills who," Yash said, his voice laced with a chilling sense of resolve. "I'm here, my dear Sasi, don't worry. I'll do anything for you. And for you too, Mom, Dad."

Yash reached into his pocket and pulled out a family photograph. He held it close to his heart, his fingers gently tracing the faces of his parents, his wife, his child.

"I'm coming for you, Sasi," he whispered, his voice filled with a mixture of love and a sense of unwavering determination.

# THE RECKONING OF TIME

The storm raged outside, a symphony of wind and rain battering against the apartment windows. Inside, the air crackled with tension, a tangible presence in the room. Yash, his body a mix of weariness and steely determination, stood facing twenty mercenaries, their faces hardened by a life of violence, their eyes reflecting the chilling reality of their mission.

He glanced back at Sasi, her unconscious form sprawled on the floor. His heart ached with a mixture of guilt and a desperate hope. He had to save her. He had to make things right.

He turned back to the mercenaries, his eyes blazing with a cold fury. The air crackled with anticipation as the battle was about to commence.

The mercenaries charged, their blades flashing, their movements a blur of aggression. Yash, his movements a blend of calculated precision and instinctive agility, met their attack head-on.

He sidestepped a lunging mercenary, his arm catching the man's wrist with a sharp, precise move. He then delivered a swift, powerful strike, sending the mercenary crashing into the wall, his body crumpling to the floor. The impact echoed through the room, a stark reminder of the power that lay within Yash.

The mercenaries, their initial confidence shaken, closed ranks, their movements a relentless, violent assault. Yash, his eyes locked on each of them, predicted their movements, his mind a whirlwind of strategy.

He used the room's furniture to his advantage, dodging attacks, using the weight of a coffee table to knock a mercenary off balance. He spun, his foot connecting with another mercenary's jaw, sending the man stumbling backward. He then maneuvered behind a heavy armchair, his movements a blur of speed and agility, avoiding a barrage of blades.

He moved like a shadow, his steps silent, his movements a symphony of power and grace.

His attacks were precise, his strikes calculated, his defenses flawless. He was a warrior, a protector, a man fueled by love and a desperate need to make things right.

He dodged a flurry of knife blows, his body twisting and turning, his movements a testament to his unwavering will. He then launched a counter-attack, his fist connecting with a mercenary's jaw, the sound of the impact reverberating through the room. The mercenary stumbled backward, his eyes wide with shock and disbelief, his hand clutching his jaw.

One by one, the mercenaries fell, their bodies crashing to the ground, their faces contorted in pain and disbelief. The air grew thick with the smell of blood, the scent of fear, and the echoes of violence. But the storm outside, as if mirroring the chaos within the apartment, intensified, its fury a chaotic symphony of wind and rain.

Yash, his movements fluid and precise, continued his relentless assault. He blocked a knife with the back of his hand, the force of the impact sending the blade flying across the room. He then seized the mercenary's wrist, his grip firm and unrelenting, and twisted the man's arm, dislocating the shoulder with a sickening crack. The mercenary screamed in pain, falling to the ground, his body contorted in agony.

Another mercenary, his eyes burning with a desperate rage, lunged forward, his blade glinting menacingly under the dim light. Yash, his movements a blur of speed and power, dodged the attack, his body a testament to his agility. He then countered, his fist connecting with the mercenary's chest, sending the man crashing backward.

Yash, his breath catching in his throat, pressed his advantage. He saw a mercenary about to strike from behind. He turned, a swift, decisive movement, and grabbed the man's arm. He twisted the man's arm, breaking the bone with a sickening crunch, and then delivered a swift, powerful kick, sending the mercenary flying across the room.

The mercenaries, their numbers dwindling, their confidence shattered, began to panic. But Yash, fueled by a sense of purpose, a desperate need to protect Sasi, fought with a ferocity that surprised even himself.

Another mercenary, a burly brute with a scarred face, charged towards Yash. He swung his arm, his blade aimed at Yash's head. Yash, his movements a blend of agility and precision, sidestepped the attack, his body a blur of motion. He then grabbed the mercenary's wrist, his grip tight and unwavering, and twisted the man's arm, dislocating the shoulder with a sickening crack. The mercenary stumbled backward, his face contorted with pain, his eyes wide with disbelief.

Yash, his heart pounding in his chest, knew he had to end the fight quickly. He noticed a mercenary standing near a tall bookshelf, his eyes fixed on Yash, his hand gripping his blade. Yash seized the opportunity. He kicked a nearby chair, sending it flying towards the mercenary, its trajectory a perfect arc. The chair struck the mercenary, knocking him off balance, the force of the impact sending the bookshelf crashing to the floor. The room was filled with a cacophony of noise, the sound of shattering wood, the clatter of books, and the screams of the mercenaries.

Aryan, his face a mask of fury, watched from the doorway. The chaos in the room, the sight of his men falling one by one, fueled his rage. He charged into the room, his eyes fixed on Yash.

Yash, his senses heightened, turned just in time to see Aryan's attack. He ducked, his body a blur of motion, and then countered, his fist connecting with Aryan's jaw.

Aryan, his face contorted with shock, stumbled backward.

But he quickly recovered, his eyes blazing with a cold fury.

"Hey," Aryan said, his voice laced with a chilling amusement. "How did you survive? I slashed you with my blade. How are you still moving?"

Yash, his body aching, his mind filled with a mixture of adrenaline and a sense of defiance, rolled over, his eyes fixed on Aryan. He grabbed Aryan's arm, his grip strong and unwavering, and punched him in the face.

Aryan stumbled backward, his eyes widening in shock, his body crashing against the wall. He quickly recovered, his rage boiling over.

"Tell me," Aryan said, his voice laced with a chilling threat. "There's no way you're this active. There's something going on. Only two things are possible. Either I hurt you a bit, or you're something else. Someone else."

While Aryan was talking, Yash, his mind sharp, his instincts honed by the urgency of the moment, understood what was happening.

"Yeah, your guess is right," Yash said, his voice a low growl, his eyes burning with a sense of defiance. "I'm not that person you beat. I'm the person who's going to beat you. And I've heard people call you a monster. Come on, show me your monster."

Aryan, his rage reaching a boiling point, charged towards Yash. The two of them, their bodies a whirlwind of motion, crashed into each other. Their fists connected with bone-crushing force, their bodies colliding with the walls, the sound of the impact echoing through the room.

They fought with a ferocity that was both terrifying and exhilarating. They were two men fueled by different forces, two men determined to win, two men whose fates were intertwined.

# THE UNVEILING

The scene shifted to the terrace, a vast expanse of concrete and steel, the storm raging above, the lightning illuminating the scene in stark, fleeting flashes.

Yash, his body bruised, his mind focused on survival, fought back. He dodged blows, he countered attacks, his movements a symphony of defiance. He was a man cornered, a man fighting for his life, a man fighting for his love.

He caught the iron rod, his grip strong, his movements a testament to his strength. He then threw the rod, its trajectory precise, its impact forceful.

The iron rod struck Aryan, sending him stumbling backward.

The two of them, their bodies a whirlwind of motion, clashed. They fought with a ferocity that was both terrifying and captivating. Their fists connected with bone-crushing force, their bodies colliding with the railing, the sound of their struggle echoing through the night.

Their fight, a symphony of violence, was a testament to the raw, untamed power that lay within them. They fought for their lives, for their love, for their futures.

Then, a sudden change in the tide of the battle.

Yash, his mind racing, saw an opportunity. He used his agility and intelligence to his advantage, his movements a blend of calculated precision and instinctive grace.

He ducked under Aryan's blow, his body a blur of motion. He then landed a powerful kick, his foot connecting with Aryan's jaw. Aryan stumbled, his eyes widening in disbelief, his body crashing into the railing.

Yash, his movements a blur of speed and power, pressed his attack. He landed a series of blows, his fists connecting with Aryan's ribs, his body a weapon of destruction.

Aryan, his face contorted with pain, his rage reaching a fever pitch, stumbled backward, his body a testament to the brutal force of Yash's attacks.

Yash, his movements fluid and precise, continued his onslaught. He delivered a final, devastating blow, his fist connecting with Aryan's jaw, the force of the impact sending Aryan crashing to the ground.

Aryan, his body limp, his face contorted with a mixture of shock and defeat, lay on the floor, his eyes fixed on Yash, a mixture of disbelief and a chilling sense of understanding playing across his features.

Yash, his body weary, his heart heavy with the weight of the battle, stood over Aryan.

Aryan, his voice a mixture of pain and a desperate need to understand, looked up at Yash.

"Oh, you fight well," Aryan said, his voice a low, raspy whisper. "But you can't kill me. And I don't care who you are. Why are you here? Why are you trying to save her? Now it's time to die."

Aryan, his hand reaching for the blade, raised his weapon, his eyes filled with a sense of chilling determination.

He was about to strike, to deliver the final blow.

But then, a sudden movement.

A knife plunged into Aryan's back.

Aryan, his body convulsing in pain, turned slowly, his eyes widening in disbelief. He looked at the figure who had struck him.

Zara, her eyes filled with a mixture of rage and a sense of deep, unyielding sorrow, stood there, the knife still clutched in her hand.

She cried, her voice a raw, gut-wrenching sob.

Aryan, his face contorted with a mixture of pain and disbelief, dropped his blade to the ground. He reached out, his hand trembling, his fingers gently tracing Zara's face.

"Zara," he whispered, his voice laced with a mixture of shock and a desperate attempt at reconciliation.

"Don't touch me," Zara said, her voice a mixture of fury and a deep sense of betrayal. "You monster!"

She lunged, her knife flashing, and plunged it into Aryan's heart.

Aryan, his body collapsing to the ground, his eyes fixed on Zara, let out a groan, his voice a mixture of pain and a desperate plea for forgiveness.

"Why, Zara?" Aryan whispered, his voice filled with a mixture of despair and a desperate attempt to understand. "Why?"

Yash, his heart heavy with a mix of sorrow and a sense of justice, stood there, watching. He had witnessed the unfolding drama, the chilling reality of his family's lives.

He slowly walked towards Zara, his movements slow, his eyes filled with a mixture of sympathy and a sense of understanding. He reached out, his hand gently taking the knife from Zara's grasp.

He then gently pushed Zara back, creating a small distance between them.

Yash and Aryan, their eyes locked, stood there, the storm raging around them, the lightning illuminating their faces in stark, fleeting flashes.

"I know, Aryan," Yash said, his voice filled with a sense of understanding. "I know you did all of this for your family. Especially for your wife."

Yash's gaze turned towards Zara, his eyes focusing on her stomach, a slight, gentle bump beneath her dress.

Aryan, his eyes widening in disbelief, could only stare.

"Zara," Aryan said, his voice a low, raspy whisper. "Are you pregnant?"

"Yeah," Yash said, his voice filled with a sense of quiet confidence. "And do you know one thing, Aryan? You asked me who I was. You know who I am."

Yash looked directly into Aryan's eyes, his gaze a blend of empathy and a chilling sense of finality.

"I'm your future daughter's husband," Yash said, his voice filled with a sense of understanding. "And you're the father of my wife, and you and Zara's daughter. Her name is Sasi."

The storm, as if mirroring the turmoil within the room, intensified. Lightning flashed, the sound of thunder reverberating through the night.

Aryan, his eyes wide with disbelief, his mind struggling to process the information, could only stare at Yash, his face a mixture of shock and a sense of deep, unfathomable regret.

"What?" Aryan whispered, his voice barely audible, his body filled with a sense of overwhelming disbelief.

Aryan, his life ebbing away, his eyes fading, sunk back into unconsciousness.

Sasi, her consciousness slowly returning, felt a searing pain in her head. She slowly opened her eyes, her vision blurred, her movements sluggish.

She followed the trail of blood and the sounds of the storm to the terrace.

Yash, his movements deliberate, walked towards the corner of the terrace, a quiet sense of determination in his steps.

Zara, her eyes filled with a mix of grief and a sense of relief, turned to Yash.

"Wait, Yash," Zara said, her voice a mixture of confusion and a desperate need for answers. "What are you going to do next? And what about Aryan? What should we do now? And why did you have a chance to kill him before, but you didn't? Why? Tell me."

Yash, his eyes fixed on the horizon, looked at Zara. He understood her questions, her need to know.

"I know," Yash said, his voice filled with a sense of understanding. "I had a chance to kill him before, but I didn't. I understood him. I understood his point of view. He was right. He was doing all of this for his family. And I wanted him to confess to you, so I kept him alive. He wasn't an evil man. He was a broken man."

Yash turned and walked towards the door, his movements filled with a sense of purpose.

A few minutes later, Yash returned.

"Goodbye, Mrs. Zara," Yash said, his voice filled with a sense of gratitude. "Thank you for everything you've done. For taking care of my wife and your future daughter."

"Yash, I have one thing on my mind," Zara said, her voice laced with a sense of unease. "The timeline has changed now. What's going to happen to the future? What if the timeline is changed forever?"

Yash, his smile a mixture of confidence and a sense of hope, nodded.

"I have an idea to rewrite the timeline," Yash said.

Yash reached into his pocket and pulled out the two Nexus watches. He held them in his hand, the broken watch and the new watch, symbols of his journey, his ambition, his love.

He merged the two watches, the two pieces of technology fusing together, their energy pulsing, their power combining.

The air crackled, the storm raging around them intensified, and the time vortex opened, a swirling portal of energy, a gateway to an unknown future.

"Goodbye, my mother-in-law," Yash said, his voice filled with a sense of love, gratitude, and a sense of unwavering hope.

Yash and Sasi, their bodies enveloped in the swirling energy of the time vortex, disappeared, their journey into the future a blur of light and motion.

The storm raged on, the city lights flickering, a testament to the chaos that had been unleashed. But in the midst of the storm, a sense of hope lingered.

Yash, his love for Sasi unwavering, his determination fueled by a sense of responsibility, had embarked on a quest to rewrite the timeline, to undo the mistakes he had made, to bring back his wife, to reclaim his future, to save his family.

His journey was far from over.

But he knew, with a certainty that defied logic, that he would succeed.

# THE NEXUS REFORGED

The time vortex, a swirling maelstrom of energy, swallowed Yash and Sasi whole. The world around them dissolved, a kaleidoscope of color and light, before they were spat out, two figures thrown into a world of vibrant chaos. They materialized on the edge of a bustling amusement park, the air thick with the scent of popcorn and cotton candy, the sound of laughter and screams a cacophony of joy.

This was the place. This was the point where their journey had gone awry, where the timeline had been irrevocably altered.

Yash, his mind racing, scanned the park, his gaze searching for the familiar landmarks, the twisted metal of a broken lamppost, the vibrant lights of a carousel, the shadows of a forgotten bench.

He carefully placed Sasi, still unconscious, against the wall of a small shop, her head resting gently against the cool brick.

"This is the place where the timeline was changed, where the problems started," Yash whispered, his voice a low rumble, his eyes fixed on the bustling crowd. "I'm going to change it again."

He looked at Sasi, his heart filled with a mixture of love and a sense of desperate hope. He reached out and gently brushed a strand of hair from her face.

Yash tied a scarf around his face, his movements swift and deliberate, masking his features. He then moved towards the crowd, his steps purposeful, his gaze fixed on a specific target.

Meanwhile, Sasi, her consciousness slowly returning, felt the familiar sting of disorientation. She sat up, her eyes wide with a mixture of confusion and a sense of desperate urgency.

She was back in the amusement park. She was back in the past.

She frantically searched her hands, her fingers tracing the emptiness of her wrist, her heart sinking with each passing second.

"Rox," she whispered, her voice laced with a mixture of fear and a desperate plea. "Rox, where's the watch? I have to get back to my timeline."

But Rox was silent.

Sasi, her heart pounding in her chest, stood up. She looked around, her eyes searching for any sign of the watch.

Suddenly, a figure emerged from the crowd.

Yash, his eyes fixed on Sasi, moved towards her. He stopped, his movements deliberate, his gaze filled with a sense of calculated precision.

He reached down and placed the Nexus watch on the ground, his fingers gently guiding it into position, his actions a silent plea.

Then, with a swift movement, he dashed towards Sasi, his body a blur of motion. He brushed past her, his presence a fleeting echo in the bustling crowd.

Yash, hidden in the crowd, watched as Sasi fell to the ground, her body crumpling under the impact of his touch. But even in her fall, Sasi's eyes were fixed on the watch, its silver surface gleaming under the amusement park lights.

"Oh, thank God, it was here," Sasi said, her voice filled with a mixture of relief and a sense of overwhelming gratitude.

She picked up the watch, her fingers tracing its smooth, cold surface, a sense of hope returning to her heart.

She activated the watch, its blue light pulsing, its energy swirling around her.

Yash watched, his heart pounding, his eyes fixed on Sasi. He knew that this was the moment, the moment that would change everything.

He picked up Sasi, his movements swift, his touch gentle, and stood there, his gaze fixed on her. He then watched, his heart filled with a mixture of love and a sense of profound hope, as Sasi activated the watch, its energy swirling around her, its power drawing her back to her own timeline.

The scene shifted, its focus turning to Sasi, her body enveloped in the swirling energy of the time vortex, her eyes closed, her face filled with a sense of both wonder and a hint of fear.

Then, a transformation.

Sasi, her body shimmering with a golden light, began to fade, her form dissolving into a mist of shimmering dust.

Yash, his heart pounding, his eyes filled with a mixture of love and a sense of overwhelming despair, watched, his body trembling slightly, as his wife vanished, her essence fading away.

But even as Sasi disappeared, Yash's smile remained, a silent testament to the depth of his love, the unwavering strength of his resolve. He reached out, his hand gently brushing her cheek, a final touch of affection.

He then turned, his gaze meeting hers for one final, heartbreaking moment. He leaned down, his lips brushing against her forehead, a final, silent kiss.

And then, he too, began to fade, his form dissolving into a shimmering mist, a testament to the power of the Nexus watch, a symbol of his love for Sasi.

The time vortex, its swirling energy a symphony of light and chaos, began to glow. The colors intensified, the light pulsating, a testament to the immense power that was being unleashed.

Then, a sudden shift. The scene faded, the time vortex dissolving, a new, altered timeline emerging.

# THE ECHO OF A DREAM

The morning light, a pale, filtered glow, filtered through the blinds, casting long shadows across Sasi's room. She awoke with a jolt, her heart pounding in her chest, her mind a jumble of confusion.

"Mrs. Sasi, wake up. It's getting late," Rox's synthesized voice said, its tone gentle yet insistent.

Sasi, her eyes wide with a mixture of shock and disbelief, sat up in bed. She looked around, her gaze searching the room, a sense of disorientation washing over her.

"What? Where am I?" Sasi asked, her voice laced with a mixture of confusion and a desperate need to understand.

She noticed that she was in her own bedroom, the familiar surroundings, the comforting scent of her home, a stark contrast to the chaos she had experienced only hours ago.

"What happened? How did I get back here?" Sasi whispered, her voice filled with a mixture of confusion and a desperate need to make sense of the events.

She remembered the apartment, the bloodstains, the terrifying attack of the mercenaries, the harrowing fight on the terrace, and the moment she had vanished, her body dissolving into a mist of shimmering dust.

She stood up, her movements stiff, her body still a little unsteady, and went to the bathroom, her gaze fixed on the mirror.

She stared at her reflection, her eyes widening in disbelief. She had aged.

"What?" Sasi whispered, her voice filled with a sense of confusion. "Why do I look older?"

She stood there, her mind racing, trying to understand, trying to make sense of the events that had unfolded. She felt a sense of unease, a nagging feeling that something was wrong.

She hurried down the stairs, her steps filled with a sense of urgency. She walked into the dining room, her heart pounding in her chest.

Her eyes widened in disbelief.

Dev and Kira, dressed in their usual attire, sat at the table. Kira, her face beaming with a mixture of love and concern, served Dev breakfast.

Sasi couldn't believe what she was seeing.

"Oh, Sasi, you're awake," Kira said, her voice filled with warmth, her smile a testament to her love. "Come here and have breakfast."

Sasi, her mind a whirlwind of confusion, walked towards the table, her movements automatic.

Kira, her smile unwavering, gestured to a chair.

Sasi, her eyes fixed on Kira and Dev, could only stare. She tried to understand, to make sense of the situation.

Dev, noticing Sasi's reaction, asked, "Dear Sasi, why do you look scared? Are you confused? Is something wrong?"

"Nothing, father-in-law," Sasi said, her voice a little shaky, her eyes darting between Kira and Dev.

Sasi started to eat, her movements mechanical, her mind still in a state of disbelief.

After breakfast, Sasi, Kira, and Dev stood in the hall.

"Dear parents-in-law, have you noticed anything? Do you remember anything?" Sasi asked, her voice a mix of urgency and a desperate need to know.

Kira and Dev stared at her, their faces filled with a mixture of confusion and a sense of growing concern. They looked at each other, unable to understand what Sasi was asking.

Kira, her gaze fixed on Sasi, reached out and placed her hand on Sasi's shoulder, her touch a blend of reassurance and a sense of growing alarm.

"Dear Sasi," Kira said, her voice filled with a gentle concern. "What happened to you this morning? Did you have a nightmare? Did you see something in your dreams?"

Kira hugged Sasi, her embrace a testament to her love and concern. But Sasi, her mind a jumble of confusion, remained lost in a world of disbelief.

The sound of a car pulling up outside the house shattered the silence.

"Oh, look, it's your son, Ryan. He's back from college," Dev said, his voice filled with a mixture of excitement and a sense of pride.

The door swung open, and Ryan, a young man in his late teens, entered the house.

"Hey, Grandpa and Grandma, how are you?" Ryan said, his face beaming with a sense of affection. He hugged his grandparents, his movements filled with a mixture of warmth and respect.

"My dear Ryan," Kira said, her voice filled with love and a sense of pride. "How is your studies?"

"It's going well, Grandparents," Ryan said, his eyes sparkling with a sense of ambition. "I'm preparing for my exams. I want to be a police officer or a detective in the future. So, I'm working hard."

Kira, her heart swelling with pride, kissed Ryan on his forehead.

Ryan noticed Sasi and walked towards her, his eyes filled with a mixture of concern and a hint of curiosity.

"How are you, Mom?" Ryan asked, his voice laced with a sense of concern. "I have a lot to tell you about what happened at college. But first, let me freshen up."

Ryan, his movements quick and energetic, hurried upstairs to his room.

Sasi, her mind reeling, could only stare.

"What the hell is happening here?" Sasi thought, her inner voice a mix of confusion and a sense of growing dread. "Is he really my son? What's happening? Am I daydreaming?"

She looked around the hall, her gaze fixed on the photo frames that adorned the walls. She saw images of her wedding to Yash, a photo of Ryan as a baby, a picture of her and Yash with Ryan, a collection of happy memories, a testament to their life together.

Sasi was shocked.

"I can't believe it," Sasi thought, her mind racing, her heart pounding with a mixture of disbelief and a growing sense of understanding. "This... all of this... happened. Something must have changed in the timeline. Or, maybe the timeline was altered. Corrected. It's back on the right track."

The sound of a motorcycle engine revving broke the silence.

Sasi recognized the sound. She hurried towards the front door, her movements filled with a mixture of anticipation and a sense of hope.

She opened the door, her eyes widening in disbelief.

Yash, wearing his helmet, got off his motorcycle and walked towards her, his eyes fixed on her face.

# CHAPTER THIRTY-FOUR

# THE REUNION

He removed his helmet, revealing his face, his smile a beacon of hope in the midst of her confusion.

Sasi and Yash stared at each other, their eyes locked in a silent exchange.

Yash, his hand outstretched, gestured for Sasi to come closer.

Sasi, her body trembling with a mixture of disbelief and an overwhelming sense of joy, threw her arms around Yash, her embrace a testament to the love that had brought them back together.

"I don't know what happened," Sasi said, her voice choked with emotion. "And I don't want to know. Because now, I have the life I dreamed of. And you, dear, you, especially you, are my husband again, Yash."

Yash, his heart filled with a sense of overwhelming joy, held Sasi tightly, his embrace filled with a sense of both gratitude and a profound sense of love.

"Sasi," Yash said, his voice filled with a mixture of happiness and a touch of playful teasing. "I've been waiting for those words for so many years. Haven't I?"

Sasi, her mind still reeling from the events of the past few days, looked at Yash, her eyes filled with a mixture of confusion and a sense of growing awareness.

"What words?" Sasi asked, her voice a little shaky.

Yash, his smile widening, looked into her eyes.

"I... love... you," Yash said, his voice filled with a sense of profound love, his words a testament to the journey that had brought them together.

Sasi's face lit up with a radiant smile. Her heart, filled with a mixture of disbelief and an overwhelming sense of joy, responded to his love.

Yash and Sasi, their lips meeting, embraced in a passionate kiss. They stood there, lost in the moment, their love a beacon of hope in a world filled with shadows and uncertainty.

They walked back inside the house, their hands intertwined, their footsteps a rhythmic counterpoint to the storm that raged outside.

A few minutes later, the family gathered around the dining table. They ate their breakfast, their laughter filling the room, their smiles a testament to the joy that had returned to their lives.

Yash and Sasi looked at each other, their eyes locked, their love a silent language that transcended words.

Then, the doorbell rang.

Sasi, her movements automatic, walked towards the door, her hand reaching for the knob.

She opened the door, her eyes widening in disbelief.

Mr. V, his face beaming with a sense of warmth and a hint of amusement, stood on the doorstep. Beside him, his wife, Ria, a woman whose face radiated a sense of warmth and kindness, stood with their two children, Yuki and Yuna. The children were the same age as Ryan, their faces a mixture of curiosity and a sense of nervous anticipation.

"May I come in, Mrs. Sasi?" Mr. V asked, his voice filled with a gentle politeness.

"Please come in, sir," Sasi said, her voice laced with a mixture of gratitude and a sense of awe.

The two families, united by a shared history and a sense of destiny, greeted each other. They took their places at the dining table, their laughter filling the room, their smiles a testament to the joy that had returned to their lives.

both Yuna,Yuki,Ryan all of them were same age , a tennages, where Yuna, her eyes fixed on Ryan, found herself blushing. Yash, observing their interaction, noticed Yuna's reaction. He couldn't help but smile, a small, knowing smile, his heart warmed by the budding connection between his son and the daughter of the man who had helped to save his life.

The scene, a vibrant tapestry of happiness and love, zoomed out, the camera slowly panning across the exterior of the house.

The sun, shining brightly, seemed to be a beacon of hope, a symbol of a future filled with promise.

But then, a gradual change. The sunlight, its intensity growing, began to darken, its golden rays morphing into a crimson glow. The sky, once a canvas of blue, became a canvas of blood red, the sun morphing into a malevolent moon.

The story ended, the scene fading, leaving the viewer with a sense of both hope and a chilling sense of foreboding.

# CHAPTER THIRTY-FIVE

# THE SYMPHONY OF SOULS

The cosmic realm shimmered with an ethereal light, a canvas of swirling nebulae and celestial dust. The air hummed with a symphony of ancient energies, a testament to the boundless power that pulsed through the universe.

The Elder God, a majestic figure cloaked in shimmering robes, sat on a throne crafted from starlight. His presence, as potent as a supernova, filled the chamber with an aura of infinite wisdom. He gazed out at the swirling cosmos, his eyes reflecting the infinite expanse of time and space.

The assistant, a young man with a mischievous glint in his eye, sat opposite the Elder God, his gaze fixed on the Elder God's face, a mixture of awe and a hint of nervousness in his eyes. He had a look of contentment on his face, a sense of quiet satisfaction emanating from him.

"So, child," the Elder God said, his voice a deep, resonating rumble that echoed through the chamber, its tones both gentle and imposing, "What's your opinion about this story? About the journey of Sasi?"

"Great One," the assistant replied, his voice filled with a mixture of awe and admiration. "The journey of Sasi and this story were magnificent. Time played a crucial role in their lives and in this tale. And previously, in that story, destiny played a crucial role. Now, it's time." The assistant smiled. "All of these stories are fascinating, my Great One."

"And, Great One," the assistant continued, his voice filled with a sense of wonder, "I've understood one thing. In both stories, women were at the heart of the tale. Why, Great One?"

The Elder God, his eyes twinkling with a sense of knowing, smiled, a knowing glint in his eyes. He leaned forward, his gaze fixed on the assistant.

"Remember, child, what is the universe without women? The universe would be incomplete. Meaningless."

The Elder God paused, allowing the weight of his words to settle.

"And," the Elder God continued, his voice filled with a profound reverence, "even more beautiful than life itself is womanhood. Like life itself, but above in terms of beauty and significance. When it comes to womanhood..."

The assistant's eyes widened, his jaw dropping slightly as he stared at the Elder God. He was speechless. The weight of the Elder God's words settled upon him, a profound truth that resonated within him.

"Wow, Great One," the assistant said, his voice filled with a sense of awe. "I accept. Without women, there is no home. There is no world. There is no universe."

"And, Great One," the assistant said, his voice filled with a sense of eager anticipation, "We have seen fantasy and sci-fi. I think we're done."

The assistant stretched his arms and legs, his body a testament to his relaxed, contented state. He yawned, a sound of fatigue, but his eyes still shone with a sense of wonder.

The Elder God chuckled softly. A low, rumbling sound that reverberated through the chamber, a sound that held a hint of amusement, but also a touch of something else, something that sent a shiver down the assistant's spine.

The assistant, his expression changing from one of contentment to a sudden sense of apprehension, raised his eyebrows.

"Wait, Great One," the assistant said, his voice laced with a hint of alarm. "That laugh... no, no, Great One. Another story? Wait, Great One. Another story? What's the genre this time?"

The Elder God, his smile widening, chuckled again.

"Listen up," the Elder God said, his voice a low, resonating rumble. "We've only seen the beginning of the story. Now, we're going to see the true conclusion. And now, we will explore the psychological horror genre, shall we, child?"

"And this next story," the Elder God continued, his voice filled with a sense of both anticipation and a touch of mystery, "will be the culmination of all the stories we have seen so far. We're going to see everyone in the same story this time."

The assistant's mind raced, his eyes widening with a mixture of disbelief and a sense of eager anticipation. He leaned forward, his gaze fixed on the Elder God.

"What, Great One?" the assistant said, his voice a mix of disbelief and a sense of growing excitement. "All the characters in one story? How is that even possible? And, Great One, what is the theme of this story? Is it about destiny or time?"

The Elder God, his smile widening, his eyes twinkling with a sense of amusement and a sense of profound knowledge, leaned forward.

"Now, we shall see the story of souls," the Elder God said, his voice filled with a sense of both mystery and a touch of a chilling foreboding.

The scene faded, the cosmic realm dissolving into a swirling vortex of light and energy. The assistant, his heart pounding with anticipation, could only wait, his mind racing, his senses heightened.

The Elder God's words, his promise of a story that would bring together all the characters, the story of souls, lingered in the air, a chilling whisper in the vast, unending universe.

The next chapter, a symphony of horror, waited to unfold.

www.ingramcontent.com/pod-product-compliance
Lightning Source LLC
Chambersburg PA
CBHW031958140726
47988CB00019B/2486